THE MYSTERIOUS FOUR

CLOCKS and ROBBERS

DAN POBLOCKI

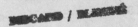

Scholastic Inc.

New York   Toronto   London   Auckland
Sydney   Mexico City   New Delhi   Hong Kong

*This book is dedicated to Kathy, my secret twin
and everlasting cheerleader.*

No part of this publication may be reproduced, stored in a retrieval system,
or transmitted in any form or by any means, electronic, mechanical,
photocopying, recording, or otherwise, without written permission of the
publisher. For information regarding permission, write to Scholastic Inc.,
Attention: Permissions Department, 557 Broadway, New York, NY 10012.

ISBN 978-0-545-29981-7

Copyright © 2011 by Dan Poblocki
All rights reserved. Published by Scholastic Inc.
SCHOLASTIC and associated logos are trademarks and/or registered
trademarks of Scholastic Inc.

12 11 10 9 8 7 6 5 4 3 2   11 12 13 14 15 16/0

Printed in the U.S.A.   40
First printing, August 2011

1

THE STRANGERS GAME

A spherical clock has sat atop a tall black iron pedestal in front of the Moon Hollow Public Library for as long as anyone can remember. The clock's large, ornately designed, four-sided face gazes unassumingly upon busy and bustling Maple Avenue, where shops, restaurants, and office buildings stand side by side like books shoved tightly onto a shelf.

One day in early November, a girl named Rosie Smithers watched from the sidewalk outside Deakin's Pharmacy as the clock's big hand leapt ahead five minutes in less than five seconds. Four loud chimes rang out and echoed up the street with stern authority.

Like the clock's pedestal, Rosie was also tall and thin. Her skin was the color of cocoa. Her hair was long, and twisted into many braids that fell to her shoulders. "Did you see that?" she asked, turning to her friend, Viola Hart. They had been waiting for Rosie's mother, the town librarian, to get out of work. Mrs. Smithers was going to take the girls to the shopping center on Oakwood Avenue so Rosie could get a new coat.

The zipper was stuck at the bottom of her old one—a hand-me-down from her older sisters.

"See what?" Viola answered. Her eyes grew wide with excitement. Viola was a smallish girl with a burst of red curls on top of her head and freckles on her pale round cheeks. Recently, she had moved next door to Rosie, and the girls had become fast friends.

"The minute hand on that big clock was stuck at three fifty-five for a while," Rosie explained. "Then, it jumped forward to four o'clock."

A couple months before, the girls had formed a mystery club called the Question Marks, with Sylvester Cho and Woodrow Knox—two boys who lived on their block. After school every few days, the club members would share with one another the small mysteries they'd encountered around town. They met at the spot where their four backyards came together—a place they called the Four Corners.

"The minute hand *jumped*?" Viola asked. "Like . . . *sproing*?" Rosie nodded. From her knapsack, Viola pulled out a black-and-white composition notebook and pen. Flipping the book open, she carefully jotted down a note.

Rosie recited what had recently become Viola's motto: "Mysteries are everywhere if you look for them."

Surprised, Viola laughed. "I was just about to say that!"

"I know." Rosie smiled. "I see that notebook, and I know what's coming."

"I'm no mystery, I guess." Viola shrugged. "But what about the clock?"

"You think?" Rosie squinted as she glanced across the street. "That *would* be a fun mystery. It's probably just broken though."

Viola raised an eyebrow.

It had been a couple weeks since the Question Marks had discovered the reasons for the creepy sounds Viola had heard coming from her basement. Since then, Viola, Rosie, Sylvester, and Woodrow had been anxious to find another mystery to solve. They'd paid attention to most every little thing—scraps of paper fluttering across the sidewalk, chalk drawings on the wall behind their school, car alarms screaming in the middle of the night. As they'd recently learned, anything might be a clue to a great big secret. In fact, that was the reason the girls were waiting for Mrs. Smithers across the street from the library.

During lunch that day, Viola had come up with a new challenge she'd named the Strangers Game. The point was to observe people they didn't know and try to guess who they were. So far, the girls had discreetly watched a young woman wearing faded jeans and a vintage parka carry a huge load of picture books out of the library. She didn't appear old enough to have kids of her own, and she definitely was not a teacher at their school. So who would the woman share picture books with? They guessed she must be a babysitter—probably a student at the college who needed some extra cash.

"I've got another one," Viola proclaimed, nodding at the library's entrance. "I see a woman who has a huge family, works really hard, loves cooking, and records talk shows during the day so she can watch them later at night."

Those details sounded vaguely familiar to Rosie . . . and very specific. "How did you figure all that out?" she asked, glancing up and down the street for someone who might fit the description.

Viola giggled as the woman who was standing at the library's entrance waved at them. "She's my next-door neighbor."

"Hey!" said Rosie, noticing her mother heading toward them across the plaza and past the broken clock. "My mom? That's cheating!"

"Well . . . just a little." Viola winked.

From the side window of the Main Street Diner, Sylvester Cho saw his friends Rosie and Viola get into Mrs. Smithers's Volkswagen. He raced out the front door, but by the time he reached the corner of Maple Avenue, the car had zoomed off in the opposite direction.

"Sylvester!" his dad called from the steps of the restaurant. "Is everything okay?"

"Yeah," Sylvester said. "I just saw my friends."

"Do you want to go with them?" asked Mr. Cho, looking guilty. "I can handle wiping down the tables by myself for a few hours."

"It's okay. I just wanted to say 'hey,' but they're already gone."

Normally, Sylvester would have leapt at the chance for a break, but today he was enjoying his time at his parents' restaurant. Since the end of the school day, he'd been playing the Strangers Game—Viola's latest challenge.

When he'd gotten to the diner, Sylvester had noticed an odd-looking man sitting alone at a booth near the back wall, drinking a cup of coffee. The man wore a black T-shirt and had a scruffy beard. His arms were covered with colorful tattoos. Sylvester immediately deduced that the man was in a biker gang. He kept watch on him in case the man made trouble. But after a few minutes, a beautiful young woman entered the diner, wearing a flowing green dress, a maroon velvet jacket, and a thick gray scarf wrapped casually around her neck. She was pushing a stroller. The man had stood up, kissed the woman, and then lifted a tiny baby from the carriage. "Did you miss your daddy?" the man said, then cooed at the infant.

Instantly, Sylvester realized that he'd been wrong about the man. Tattoos and a beard didn't

5

mean he was a bad guy . . . or even that he rode a motorcycle. In fact, when the family stood to go, Sylvester noticed the man grab a satchel from under the table. A logo on it read: *Hudson Valley Country Day School*. Paintbrushes, pencils, and rolled-up paper poked out from the bag's canvas flap. The man was obviously an artist—and probably a teacher!

Sylvester couldn't wait to tell his friends what he'd learned: Sometimes people are not what they appear to be.

Back inside the diner, the phone rang. Mr. Cho answered it. "Hi, honey." It was Sylvester's mother, who had taken his baby sister, Gwen, to visit his grandmother, Hal-muh-ni, just outside of New York City. Two years ago, his *ha-ra-buh-ji* had passed away, leaving his *hal-muh-ni* alone in the house where they'd raised their family.

Listening in on his parents' conversation, Sylvester started to rearrange plates on a nearby table. Behind the long counter, his father turned his back and edged away from him, tensing up. Sylvester paid even closer attention as his father lowered his voice, saying, "She agreed? Today? Uh-huh. Well, that's great news." Mr. Cho glanced at Sylvester, who quickly looked back at the table he was pretending to clean. "No," he continued, in an even lower voice. "I haven't mentioned it to him yet."

Now Sylvester was even more curious.

6

Mr. Cho hung up the phone and turned back to Sylvester. "I assume you heard all that?" he asked. Sylvester nodded. "So, what do you think?" his father asked.

"About?" Sylvester said. Should he have known what his father meant? Had he missed a clue?

"About your grandmother coming to live with us."

"Hal-muh-ni?" said Sylvester, immediately thinking how cool that would be. Then another thought popped into his head. "But where will she stay?" Their house had three bedrooms, and currently each one was taken.

Mr. Cho was silent for a few seconds. "We were thinking she would stay in your room."

"My room?" Sylvester said.

"We can fix up the basement for you instead. Your own private spot. Sound good?"

"You want me to move into . . . the *basement*?"

From behind the counter, Sylvester's father stared back at him with an uncomfortable smile. How long had his parents been planning this? How long had they kept this secret? And how could they do this to him . . . shove him away in a dark corner of the house, like an unfortunate character in a creepy fantasy story by Roald Dahl or Lemony Snicket or Neil Gaiman? Sure, having his own private spot might be interesting, but after what the Question Marks had been through in the past couple of months, he knew how disturbing a basement could be. Sylvester reached out and rearranged some silverware on a nearby table. He suddenly realized he'd been right: Sometimes people are not what they appear to be—even people you've known all your life.

That morning, Woodrow Knox's mom had asked him to come home after school and straighten up the house. Woodrow had a habit of leaving his stuff in scattered places—comic books in the living room, video games in the den, schoolwork on the kitchen table, sports equipment on the floor. His mom had said she would have a surprise for him that evening, and as Woodrow worked, he wondered what it might be. He was hoping for a flat-screen television, or maybe a new computer monitor, one that was equipped with a camera so he could chat over the Internet with his dad, who lived in Manhattan.

Woodrow was nearly finished tucking his little messes out of sight when loud chimes sounded from the center of town. Five o'clock. Mrs. Knox would be home soon from her job with the park service in the hills outside Moon Hollow. His heart pounded with anticipation. Mrs. Knox never made a very big deal out of anything, so he knew the surprise would be huge.

He was playing video games when he heard the car pull into the driveway. Quickly, he hit pause, then rushed to the front door. Swinging it open, Woodrow noticed not one car parked in front of the garage, but two. Behind his mother's forest green SUV was a bright red MINI Cooper. A man got out of it and rushed to open his mom's door. Mrs. Knox hopped out of her own car, then nodded toward Woodrow, who stood on the front porch. The man turned, smiled at him, and waved.

Woodrow blinked, contemplating what this might mean. Viola's new contest, the Strangers Game, popped into his head. *Notice the details of this man. Figure out who he is.* The man was tall. He wore a tweed jacket, a fuzzy auburn sweater, and dark blue jeans. His sandy blond hair was close-cropped and combed tightly to the side. Obviously, the man was *not* here to deliver a flat-screen television . . . or anything else for that matter. His car was barely big enough to fit another person inside it; he probably didn't have any kids. He was dressed well—too well, as if he wanted to impress someone. As they came up the front walkway toward Woodrow, the man lightly touched his mom's elbow. They were smiling in an unnatural way—showing too much teeth. Woodrow had seen his mom wear the same expression the day she had interviewed for her current job. He realized what those smiles meant: These people were terrified.

Suddenly, Woodrow felt queasy. He could deal

with the surprise not being what he'd hoped. Easy. You can't mourn a television that never belonged to you. But he wasn't sure if he was ready to meet his mom's new boyfriend. And all the signs indicated that this stranger on the front walk was his mom's big surprise.

"Woodrow," said his mom, leading the tall man up the stairs, "I want you to meet my friend Bill. We're all going to have dinner here tonight. Together."

From the porch stairs, Bill extended his hand. "Nice to meet you, Woodrow. Your mom's a pretty cool lady." Mrs. Knox laughed, a little too loudly.

"I know that," said Woodrow, shaking Bill's hand like his father had taught him. He squeezed hard. "Nice to meet you too."

Woodrow wasn't sure if he liked Viola's new game. Maybe sometimes strangers should remain strangers?

Even so, he wanted to tell Sylvester, Rosie, and Viola about this. Maybe they could help him figure out more. He knew it was only a matter of time before they all met again.

As it turned out, the next morning, Woodrow got his wish.

2

THE CLOCKS OF MOON HOLLOW
(A ?????? MYSTERY)

"Did the Strangers Game work?" Standing in the center of the Four Corners, Viola Hart was bundled in a bright green puffy coat. The weather was changing. The wind rattled bare branches, and what was left of the fallen leaves *scritch*ed and *scratch*ed along the nearby streets. Surrounding Viola, the rest of the group wore heavier coats than they had the day before. Rosie's was brand-new and bubble-gum pink.

Sylvester told his story of the tattooed man, about how Sylvester's assumptions had been wrong. "That's a really great thing to notice," said Viola, impressed.

Rosie agreed. "We should all remember that. Don't judge a book by its cover . . . right?"

Then Sylvester continued. His mother had returned with his grandmother last night. His parents had set up a temporary place for him to sleep on the couch in the living room, while Hal-muh-ni stayed in his bedroom as planned. As soon as the movers brought some of her things up from her old house, his parents would bring Sylvester's bed to the basement.

"That's freaking cool, dude," said Woodrow. "We can build all sorts of secret lairs down there."

"I don't really want my room to be a secret lair."

Woodrow simply stared at him, as if he couldn't believe what he was hearing.

"It sounds like your grandmother needs your help," said Rosie. "You're being really generous. My brothers and sisters and I have to share all sorts of things in my house. It's annoying, but we make it work. Well, mostly." Sylvester nodded, but he wasn't enthusiastic about it.

Woodrow went next, telling them about dinner the night before. Bill had ended up cooking a rosemary-herbed pork loin, with a side of steamed turnip greens. Woodrow had enjoyed the meat, but barely managed to choke down the soggy vegetables. "Who actually *eats* turnip greens?" he said.

"I like them all right," Rosie said quietly.

"Turnip greens?" said Sylvester, shuddering. "I've never heard of them, and I don't think I want to."

"What does Bill do for a living?" Viola asked.

"He has some big job at the bank up on Maple. The one right next to that boarded-up storefront."

"Did you like him?" Viola asked Woodrow.

"I guess he was nice enough. But I don't trust him. I just know there's something wrong with him."

"Why?" said Viola, ready to open her ever-present notebook.

Woodrow thought for a moment. "I can't place my finger on it."

"I guess you should wait, then," Viola answered cautiously. "See what clues come up." She didn't want to hurt his feelings by saying he might be wrong.

"Maybe you're right," said Woodrow, glancing back at his house longingly, as if another, better surprise might be waiting for him inside when he returned.

"So nobody has anything else?" said Viola. "No *mysteries*?"

Rosie raised her hand. "There *was* the thing with the clock. . . ."

"I thought you said it was just broken," Viola said.

"It might be worth mentioning." Rosie nodded at the boys. Sylvester and Woodrow stared at her intently. She told them what she'd noticed yesterday when she and Viola were waiting in front of the library—about how the minute hand had leapt forward.

"That's funny," said Woodrow. "There's another clock just like that one down at the train

13

station, next to the platform. I've noticed it when I've gone to visit my dad, but I've never seen it do anything odd."

"What does it look like?" asked Sylvester.

"Just like the one on Maple Avenue, like a big black Tootsie Pop, you know, with a bulbous head on top of a tall skinny pedestal. I'm sure you've seen it. It has four faces, staring out from the bulb in four directions."

Viola wrote in her notebook as Woodrow continued. "The clock by the train station is really cool. Just below the center of each face where the two hands meet, there's a little half-moon window. In the window, a series of miniature pictures rotates through so that only one is showing at a time. I've seen a leaf, I think, and a cherry."

"The one in front of the library is the same!" said Viola. "Yesterday, I noticed a small acorn peeking out from the window."

"What could that mean?" said Sylvester.

"It could just be part of the design," Rosie answered. "Not everything has to mean something." She quickly glanced at Viola, hoping she hadn't hurt her friend's feelings.

Viola pursed her lips, but nodded. "You're right. But maybe we should all take a walk down to the train station and check out the other clock too. You know . . . just in case?"

With nothing else planned for Saturday morning, the group let their parents know where they were going before setting off down the hill.

The train station on Oakwood Avenue was a quaint stone building that stood next to the tracks. The station's doors were painted deep green. Its pitched roof was made of old slate, varnished wood, and tarnished copper. A large portion of it hung over the platform, providing shade to whoever stood on the cobblestone patio below.

The clock was exactly as Woodrow had described it—a twin of the one in front of Moon Hollow Public Library. Near the bottom of each face, a name had been printed in an elaborate and frilly type. *P. W. Clintock.* Today, the image showing through the half-moon windows was a bright green leaf.

"That's from a maple tree," said Rosie. "Like on the Canadian flag."

"So you think these clocks were made by Canadians?" asked Sylvester.

"Does it matter?" said Woodrow.

"I don't know! Viola's always saying 'mysteries are everywhere if you look for them.'"

"This is a mystery, then?" Rosie asked. "Two clocks that look exactly the same in two different parts of town?"

"Well . . . ," said Viola. "What makes a mystery? How do we know we've found one?" The group thought for a second.

"Something is out of place?" Rosie suggested. "Or lost or stolen . . . or just plain odd."

"Mm-hm," said Viola. "The question is: How odd are these clocks?"

"Whoa!" Sylvester shouted, pointing at the clock. "Did you see that?" Everyone in the group turned. "The minute hand jumped forward!"

Viola quickly pulled her notebook out of her coat pocket. "What number was it stuck at before it jumped?"

"I don't know," said Sylvester, thinking. The time now read 11:25. "Maybe eleven twenty?"

"So it jumped five minutes. Just like yesterday at the library." Viola wrote all of this down.

Woodrow chuckled. "Does that answer your question?

"Which question?" said Viola.

"About how *odd* these clocks are . . ."

Rosie smiled. "You guys, I think we might have found the beginning of another mystery."

They sat on one of the benches and watched the clock for another twenty minutes, but the large hand did not jump forward again. Eventually, Rosie suggested they hike over to the library and examine the other clock together.

By the time they reached the library's plaza, almost an hour had passed since they'd arrived at the train station.

"Check it out," said Sylvester. "The maple leaf is showing on this clock too."

They surrounded the clock so that each of them could see one of its four faces. Each face showed the leaf. "Interesting," said Viola. "They must be on the same schedule."

"I wonder . . ." Woodrow looked at his watch, comparing his time to the clock's. "I think the clock's stuck at twelve twenty. The large hands haven't moved since we got here, and my watch says it's almost—"

"There it goes!" Viola shouted. All four of them finally saw the minute hand leap forward. It landed on the number five, just like the one at the train station had done an hour ago. They stared at each other in shock for several seconds. "You can't say that doesn't mean something," said Viola.

"Yesterday," Rosie began, "the clock paused on the eleven before jumping forward to the twelve. Maybe the minute hand gets stuck on the same number every hour, a different number every day?"

"We'll have to test out that theory," said Viola, continuing to take notes. "We've got some time."

"An hour," said Sylvester, "to be exact."

"You said that yesterday the picture on the clock was an acorn," Woodrow mentioned to Viola. "Today it's a maple leaf. Could it be a metaphor for something?"

"Yeah, like . . . for . . . growth?" said Sylvester. "Don't acorns grow up into maple trees?"

"No." Rosie shook her head. "Acorns grow up into oak trees."

Sylvester looked embarrassed. "Well, maybe the images are connected in a way. What do a cherry, a maple leaf, and an acorn have in common?"

"They're all plants?" Woodrow suggested.

Viola raised her hand. "I think the pictures might be a great aspect to explore later. But right now, we've overlooked an obvious, solid clue that can lead us down a very specific path. As long as we're right here at the library . . . Who wants to find out who this P. W. Clintock is?"

The library was a stone building, built in the early 1920s. Inside, reaching up to the high ceiling, various golden sculptures decorated the polished marble walls. At the far left of one wall, a farmer held a small scythe. He pointed at a calf who stood beside him. The calf craned its neck up to look above them at a grand eagle with wide wings. The eagle appeared to be eyeing a kneeling robed woman who held a salmon she'd caught from a nearby stream. The sculptures looked like something out of an old history textbook.

There was a marker on one wall describing the artwork and the artist, a local woman Viola had never heard of before. The sculptures had struck her the first time she'd visited the library a couple months ago, and every time since, she'd seen something new. Today, she noticed the small image of a sundial, which was located on the far right side of the wall.

Why did time suddenly seem so important here in Moon Hollow?

The group signed up for a computer. Searching the Internet, they learned that Paul Winston Clintock had been a local clockmaker. His factory sat on the river just north of Moon Hollow, but the company had shut their doors in the early 1990s. Rather than continue the business when Mr. Clintock had passed away, his heirs decided to sell the machinery and the building itself. On another website, the group discovered that the old factory had been converted into an apartment building. On a third site, they learned that Mr. Clintock had been a philanthropist—a generous person who used his wealth to aid others. He had helped to pay for the construction of the Moon Hollow Theatre. He had started a scholarship fund for needy students. He had donated three clocks to the town—the one in front of the library, the one next to the train station, and one more, across the street from the entrance of Moon Hollow College, on Cherry Tree Lane. He had also given several donations to the town library. The library had even named a room after him—the Clintock Gallery.

"I know where that room is," said Rosie.

"Show us," said Viola, getting excited.

The group followed Rosie back into the lobby, then through a doorway into a long room, like a wide hallway with dark wood walls. A brass plaque bolted next to the door told them they were in the right place. *"The Clintock Gallery. Moon Hollow thanks our friends for their generosity,"* Viola read from the plaque's small text. Along one side of the room, several photographs hung, portraits of serious-looking men and women, dressed in clothes from decades past.

"Who are these people?" asked Sylvester, as his eyes roamed from picture to picture.

"'Our friends'?" Rosie suggested.

"Look," said Woodrow, "their names are printed on tiny markers on each frame." He pointed at the top right photograph. "There's Mr. Clintock himself." The man in the picture had a skinny face with a long gray goatee. He wore a dark suit, wide circular spectacles, and a wry smile, like the *Mona Lisa's.* "And these are some other people who must have made donations to the town."

"Check that out." Viola pointed at more words,

engraved on a large brass plate above the wall of photographs. *"The First Principles,"* she read. "What's that supposed to mean?"

"I think it's referring to these," said Woodrow. Above each photo was a smaller metal marker, each containing a single word. In order, they read:

TRUTH	IDEALISM	MERIT
ETERNITY	KNOWLEDGE	EXEMPLAR
EMPATHY	PURITY	EVOLUTION
REASON	SERVICE	

"Maybe each of these 'principles' is a trait of the person," he said.

"But what a strange thing for the library to do," said Rosie. "I feel like there's more to it."

"Maybe your mom knows something else about this gallery," Viola said. "Why don't you ask her tonight?"

Whether they wanted to or not, each of the four had obligations outside of detective work throughout the week that followed.

The next Saturday afternoon, Viola invited everyone to tag along with her father to go see the third clock, on Cherry Tree Lane, across the street from the great stone wall and gatehouse that marked the entrance to Moon Hollow College. While Mr. Hart attended a meeting on campus, the four stayed behind to examine the clock, which stood several feet from the curb upon a small brick patio.

"This clock is exactly the same as the other two," said Woodrow. "As . . . you . . . can clearly see." He blushed.

Sylvester snorted, trying to contain his laughter.

Viola said, "But look: The picture in the little window is a cherry."

"Yesterday," said Rosie, "at the library, I noticed the image was the same as last Saturday—it was still a maple leaf. Then, this morning, I was helping my mom run some errands. We drove up Maple Avenue, and I noticed the picture on that clock had changed to the cherry."

"The images on each clock must turn at the same time," said Viola. "I think it's also safe to assume that they rotate on a weekly basis— every Saturday morning. That seems to be when we've noticed the difference."

"Yeah," said Woodrow. "And the numbers where the minute hands get stuck change too. On Friday of last week, they were on the eleven. Since last Saturday morning they've been sticking at the four. I wonder what the number will be today?"

"We can wait here to find out," said Rosie. "It *should* take less than an hour."

In the meantime, Sylvester shared that he'd officially moved into his family's basement, since his grandmother's belongings had arrived in the middle of the week. She hadn't brought too many things with her from her old house. The ugliest item was an old ratty couch, which his mother hated. It was bright yellow and the cushions were puffy crushed velvet. Sylvester agreed with his mom—it was bizarre!—but Hal-muh-ni insisted they make room for it.

"She must really like that couch," said Woodrow.

"I guess." Sylvester shrugged. "Old people are so weird." Rosie threw him a dirty look. "Sorry," he said quickly, "I mean they are so . . . *particular.*"

"Bam!" Viola shouted, pointing at the clock. "The minute hand was stuck at seven minutes past the hour—between the one and the two. It just jumped ahead five minutes."

"Okay," said Rosie. "This is definitely not a coincidence."

"There's a definite pattern," Viola agreed, wandering around the clock, looking at it from all angles. Then, she flinched, as if she'd been struck by a bolt of lightning. "Wait a second!" She opened her notebook and flipped through the last few pages. "I didn't think of it until I actually saw the image of the cherry here today. The three images aren't just random nature pictures. The cherry, the acorn, and the leaf. They *do* mean something. And it has to do with where we're standing."

"We're surrounded by plants," suggested Sylvester, nodding at the forest past the small stone wall. "Maybe they're the same kind of plants that we noticed on the clocks."

"I don't think so." Viola shook her head. "It's something else. ***Does anyone else want to guess?***"

The group stared at Viola in confusion. "Oh, come on!" she said, waving her arms wide. "What street are we standing on?"

"Oh my gosh!" said Rosie. "Cherry Tree Lane!"

Sylvester still looked confused. "So? What does this street have to do with the clocks?"

Woodrow nudged Sylvester in the shoulder. "The symbols . . . They represent where each clock stands."

"A cherry, a maple leaf, and an acorn?" Sylvester tried to work through it. Finally, it all clicked, and he gasped. "Oh yeah, Cherry Tree Lane. Here we are. And the clock in front of the library is on Maple Avenue. Weird! But what about the acorn? I don't know any street in this town called *Acorn*."

"Uh-huh," said Rosie. "But an acorn doesn't stay an acorn. *Which street around here might be represented by an acorn?*"

"Well, thanks to you, I now recognize that an acorn grows into *oak* tree," Sylvester said with a smirk. "Oakwood Avenue! That's where the train station is."

"Nice job," said Woodrow. Sylvester nodded a modest *thank-you*.

"So we know what the symbols represent," Rosie said. "But there's another part of this puzzle we haven't considered yet."

"The numbers?" said Viola.

"Exactly. This whole thing is starting to seem like a code, don't you think? It's as if Mr. Clintock was sending out a message to someone in the town using his clocks. I'm pretty sure the numbers are just as significant as the symbols."

"In what way?" asked Sylvester.

Woodrow glanced up and down the street. Beyond the campus wall, college students were wandering in groups, chattering loudly, their voices echoing past the stone gatehouse. He snapped his fingers. "We've already figured out that the symbols represent different roads in Moon Hollow, so if the numbers mean something too, they could be related to those streets."

"Hey, I know!" said Sylvester. "The numbers are a locker combination!"

"But which locker?" said Rosie. "How would we find it?"

Woodrow smiled at the group, teasing them with another question. "You guys aren't listening to me. . . . *If what we've found is actually a code, how would the series of numbers correspond with Mr. Clintock's symbols for the streets of Moon Hollow?"*

"They're addresses," said Viola.

"That's exactly what I was thinking!" said Woodrow.

"Hold on," said Rosie. "In the last week or so, we've seen the minute hands stuck at the eleven and the four. Those numbers make sense as addresses. But today it was stuck in between the one and the two."

"Can an address be one and a half?" asked Sylvester.

"You're thinking in terms of the numbers that are written on the clock faces," said Viola. "Those numbers represent the hour. But you should be thinking smaller. *What other numbers might the hand be pointing us to?*"

Rosie snapped her fingers. "It's the minute hand that sticks. So we should be thinking in terms of the minutes, not the hours!"

"Right," Viola said. "So the minute hand pointing to the number eleven on a clock face translates to fifty-five."

"I get it now," said Sylvester. "The four on a clock is at the twenty-minute mark."

"And we're not looking for one-and-a-half Cherry Tree Lane," said Viola. "The clock was stuck at *seven* minutes past."

Woodrow pointed across the street. "Look at the gatehouse. The entry's address is posted in bright green copper right there on the side of the building: Number Seven Cherry Tree Lane."

"Whoa," said Viola, Rosie, and Sylvester at the exact same time.

"If it *is* a code," said Woodrow, "right now, it's pointing at this spot." He glanced up and down the street. "What are we supposed to be looking for?"

After their discovery, the Question Marks were eager to learn the locations of the other addresses hidden in Mr. Clintock's code: fifty-five and twenty. When Mr. Hart finished with his meeting, he found the group where he'd left them outside the campus. They all piled into his car, and he drove them home.

The kids raced into Viola's house, to the den where the family's computer sat. They had their answer in no time. "Well, that was obvious!" said Viola. "The library is at *fifty-five* Maple Avenue. And the train station is at *twenty* Oakwood Avenue."

"I don't get it," said Rosie. "Why would P. W. Clintock mark the addresses of these three buildings within the clockworks he donated to the town?"

"Good question," said Viola, leaning back in the desk chair where she sat. "I also wonder why the addresses change every week."

"Yeah," said Sylvester. "And if he *was* sending out a message, who was it for?"

"Hmm," Woodrow said. He was sitting on the floor next to Viola. He tapped his fingers on the metal desk's legs. "We do have another path to search. Rosie, did your mom ever find out anything else about those people whose pictures are in the Clintock Gallery at the library?"

"No. She said she hasn't had time."

"Fine." Woodrow stood up. "We can do it ourselves instead."

The group asked Mrs. Hart to drop them off in front of the library, and she was happy to oblige. She had work to do at home and wanted some quiet.

The four wandered around the library clock for a short while, watching it as if it might reveal another clue to them. The cherry shone brightly from the opening below the clock's hands.

Inside, the group headed to the Clintock Gallery, where the eleven portraits hung on the wall. In her notebook, Viola recorded the names of the people in the pictures. "At least now we know what their names are," she said. "We should probably figure out what they did. Let's go look them up."

Rosie led everyone toward the computer room, but Sylvester hung back. "We already know what they did," he answered. "It says it on the wall." He pointed at the brass plate that read *The First Principles*. "They were school principals."

Woodrow laughed and called down the hall. "No, they weren't. You're talking about two different words, spelled two different ways. 'A principal is your *pal*' . . . We learned that in, like, first grade. Remember?"

Sylvester blushed and ran to catch up with the rest of them. "Never mind," he muttered.

Rosie was able to finagle her way into getting two computers for the four of them. She and Viola worked on one, Woodrow and Sylvester used the other. They divided the list of names and were able to uncover the identity of most of the people in the portraits. When they were finished, the four came back together at one of the circular tables near the computer desks and shared what they had learned.

"They each have two things in common," Viola said. "The first is that they were all wealthy members of the Moon Hollow community during the twentieth century—bankers, lawyers, a professor, an heiress, an artist, a politician. The second is . . . they're all dead."

"That's really creepy," said Sylvester. He shuddered. "Do you think someone murdered all of them?"

Viola shook her head emphatically. "It's much simpler than that. Judging by their birth dates, what happened to them was natural. They grew old."

"Are their pictures on the wall simply because they were generous?" Rosie asked. "Or are they connected more specifically to Mr. Clintock and his clocks?"

The group was quiet for a moment, considering Rosie's question.

"Maybe the answer lies in the words on each of the picture frames," Viola said. "Truth. Idealism. Merit. Eternity. *The First Principles*. Do they tell us anything else about how they were connected?"

Woodrow jolted upright and slammed his hand on the table. The large room went silent as all eyes suddenly turned on the group of four kids. "Sorry," Woodrow whispered, "but what Viola just said gave me an idea."

"Well . . . are you going to tell us?" asked Sylvester, leaning forward.

"If Mr. Clintock embedded a message in the clocks he donated to the town," Woodrow said, "it would make sense that he might leave messages in other places too, don't you think?"

"Sure," said Viola, starting to clue in.

"That gallery is named the Clintock Gallery, right?" said Woodrow. "So, it's likely that Mr. Clintock had some control over whose pictures hung there, what words would be associated with each photo, and even what the group of portraits would be called." Woodrow paused and bit at his lip. "I think that *The First Principles* isn't just a title for the portrait series. It's a clue about how to decode another secret message."

"Another secret message?" echoed Rosie. "What do you mean?"

"Like an anagram?" asked Sylvester.

"Sort of," said Woodrow. "This one *is* another play on letters. Use the clue 'The *First* Principles.' And think about each word associated with the portraits in the Clintock Gallery. ***Can you puzzle out Mr. Clintock's second message?***"

Sylvester, Rosie, and Viola sat at the table racking their brains. Woodrow leaned back and watched. Viola had her notebook lying open and was scribbling furiously. Together, the three whispered and fretted until finally they looked up, satisfied. "The First Principles," said Viola, "tells us to look at the *first letters* in each word. Truth. Idealism. Merit. Eternity. When we look at their first letters only, we get a new word: *time.*"

"Exactly!" said Woodrow. "Nice work, you guys."

"You were the one who figured out the code," said Sylvester, patting his friend's shoulder.

"So what's the rest of the message?" Woodrow added.

Rosie read the last part aloud. "Knowledge. Exemplar. Empathy. Purity. Evolution. Reason. Service. The first letter of each spells out: *keepers.*"

"Timekeepers?" said Viola, shaking her head. "What have we stumbled on here?"

Rosie glanced over her shoulder at the computer desk. She nodded. "Let's find out." The group followed Rosie and gathered around a single screen. This time, she entered the word *timekeepers* into the Internet search engine. There were way too many solutions to even begin looking through. "We need to narrow the search."

"How about trying *Moon Hollow* and *time-keepers*," said Viola.

When Rosie searched again using Viola's suggestion, she gasped at the result. The first website that popped up had to do with obscure secret societies. She quickly read through it. "According to this site, in the mid-twentieth century, there existed a little-known social club right here. They called themselves The Timekeepers of Moon Hollow. But no one knows who the members were."

"I don't believe it," said Viola in wonder. "Did we just uncover the identities of an old secret society in *this* town? Could the members be the people whose pictures are hanging on the wall in the other room?"

"That's got to be who they are," said Sylvester. "Wow."

Rosie turned to the group. "What exactly is a secret society?"

"My grandfather was a member of the Masons, a really famous secret society," said Viola. "The societies are kind of like any fraternity or sorority at a college. Basically, they are organizations who keep their goings-on . . . well . . . secret."

"Why?" Rosie asked. "Are they doing illegal stuff?"

"I don't think so," said Viola. "My grandfather

was a pretty normal guy. I think mostly, his group was a bunch of close friends."

Sylvester nodded. "I've heard that most secret societies are people who help other people."

"Like what the Kiwanis Club does here in town?" said Rosie. "My sister got a scholarship from them a couple years ago to attend a leadership camp at Moon Hollow College."

"Or . . . like us," said Sylvester. "The Question Marks help people too." The group chuckled. "What?" he continued, offended. "We solve mysteries!"

"You're right," said Viola. "It's funny to think of ourselves as a secret society . . . but we are, in a way." After a moment, she continued. *The First Principles* might be a series of the Timekeepers' beliefs. Maybe those words are not *only* a code but also a type of . . . motto."

"That's a possibility," said Woodrow. "The words do represent good qualities. We already know that the members of the group were generous. Mr. Clintock donated his fancy clocks to the town. The others gave Moon Hollow some of their money to help build this library."

"Nice of them," said Rosie.

"Who knows what else they did?" said Sylvester. "Hey, Viola, maybe we should tell your mom what we found. About the clocks and the codes. She could run an article in the *Moon*

Hollow Herald about the clocks and the Timekeepers. Wouldn't that be cool?"

"Oh, definitely," said Viola. "This is right up her alley."

Outside, the November sky was overcast. The light was dimming. When the group left the library to walk back to their block, they passed by the large clock once more. Sylvester piped up. "So, now we know who Mr. Clintock's secret messages were directed at. The Timekeepers of Moon Hollow. But there's one thing I still don't understand." He pointed at the clock. "The numbers. The symbols. The addresses. Those were his codes. They change on a weekly basis. So what? ***What exactly was he trying to tell the secret society?***"

"A club needs a meeting place," said Viola. "Right?"

"Yeah," said Rosie, zipping her coat up to her neck, protecting herself against the cold wind. "Like the Four Corners in our backyards."

"But maybe the Timekeepers had more than one meeting place," said Viola.

"Totally!" said Woodrow. "Three addresses. Three different spots to get together. The library. The train station. And the gatehouse up at the college."

"The locations rotated on a weekly basis," Viola continued. "Mr. Clintock must have set up his clocks as a reminder to the group, in a variety of locations around Moon Hollow, so each member had easy access to find out where the meeting was going to be held that week."

"They only had to glance at any of the clocks," said Rosie, "and they'd have their answer. That's so clever!"

Walking back to their block, they all secretly knew that the Question Marks had once again been pretty clever themselves.

3

THE SENSATIONAL FOUR

Mrs. Hart ran the article on Monday morning. That afternoon, Viola received a phone call from a woman claiming to be from the Associated Press. She asked to speak with Viola's mom to see if it would be okay to contact the rest of the group. The reporter, who introduced herself as Darlene Reese, wanted to run a story about the four kids who had uncovered the secrets of the little known philanthropic group in Moon Hollow, New York, known as the Timekeepers.

Rinsing lettuce in the sink for dinner, Viola could barely contain herself, she was so ecstatic. The four of them were about to become famous!

"I don't know if it's such a good idea," said Mrs. Hart.

Viola felt as though her mom had just popped a balloon.

Thankfully, her father spoke up from his office. "They deserve the attention," he called out down the hallway. "I'm really proud of you guys. Those clocks have been around town for how long ... and no one else has thought to look closer?"

"I'm not saying they're undeserving," said Mrs. Hart. "I just don't know if I want Viola's name plastered across the Internet. The *Moon Hollow Herald* is one thing . . . but the Associated Press is huge. Who knows what kinds of people pick up on these things?"

Mr. Hart wandered into the kitchen. "Well . . . what does Viola want to do?"

"I suppose I should ask my friends," Viola said. In her mind though, she shouted, *I want to talk to the reporter!*

It turned out that the rest of the group felt the same way. Later, after asking permission from their parents, Viola, Rosie, Woodrow, and Sylvester video-chatted with Darlene from the Harts' computer. The reporter asked them about their experience, and they told her a little bit about the mystery club. But after the conversation ended, Woodrow looked upset.

"What's wrong?" asked Sylvester.

Woodrow sighed. "I thought the coolest part about the Timekeepers was that they kept themselves a secret for so long. Now everyone is going to know about us: the Question Marks."

The others glanced at one another, trying to gauge if they all felt the same way. Finally, Viola spoke up. "We never said what we were doing was a secret. Maybe after this, people will come to us with even more mysteries to solve. I mean, other than the clocks case, things have been slow lately."

Woodrow still didn't look convinced.

"Don't worry about it, dude," said Sylvester, turning toward Woodrow. "This isn't going to keep all the cute girls from staring at you. In fact, they'll probably start staring at *me* too."

Rosie and Viola crossed their arms and rolled their eyes.

4

THE BUNGLING BARGAIN HUNTER
(A ??? MYSTERY)

By the time Mrs. Hart's news article appeared on the *Herald*'s website on Wednesday, the group had a couple reasons to get together other than to talk about their impending fame. They had some more mysterious stories to share.

The sun had been going down earlier and earlier. The air was too cold for them to meet at the Four Corners for an extended time anymore. So, Sylvester invited them to join him in his new bedroom.

The basement was unfinished—cinderblock walls, wood-plank stairs, storage shelves in the far dark corners. It was damp and smelled a bit like stale laundry. Hal-muh-ni's old yellow couch sat against the wall. She had also given Sylvester her big Oriental rug so that he wouldn't have to walk barefoot on the concrete floors. To him, it was very little consolation for being pushed out of his bedroom.

The four sat down on the plush fibers amid the intricately swirling and colorful patterns next to Sylvester's bed.

"Who's up first?" said Viola.

Rosie raised her hand. "This one comes from my oldest sister, Grace," she began. "Over the summer, she took a part-time job at a boutique at the shopping center on Oakwood Avenue.

"One of her favorite parts of the job is watching for shoplifters. She thinks it's fun to bust them. Once, she told me how she noticed two women with a huge shopping bag standing in a corner of the store near a pile of jeans. They kept glancing at her in a weird way. Grace noticed that it would have been really easy for them to simply slide the pile off the display table into their big bag and walk out of the store. So she immediately went over to the women and asked if she could help them. They said no, but Grace continued to stand there with her arms folded. The women got so mad they stormed out."

"Ha!" said Sylvester. "Your sister is *so* tough."

"She might be tough," said Rosie, "but that didn't help her last night."

"Oh no," said Viola. "What happened?"

"According to Grace, it had been a really busy evening. She was working at the cash register. One young woman came up, smiled, and plopped a bunch of merchandise on the counter. Before Grace could ring her up, the store manager, Tori, tapped her shoulder and pulled her aside. Out of earshot of anyone else, Tori mentioned that she'd heard that this woman was trouble. She'd recently been caught in some other local stores trying to steal stuff. Tori told Grace to be careful. My sister was feeling pretty confident, so she agreed and returned to the register.

"The shopper was nothing but pleasant. As Grace chatted with her, she kept her eyes peeled, in case the woman tried to slip something into her pocket. By the time Grace had placed every item into a shopping bag, she was certain that whatever this woman had been accused of must have been a mistake. The woman seemed completely ordinary.

"Grace gave her the total. It was almost five hundred dollars. The woman handed over her credit card. Grace ran it through the machine without a problem. The woman signed the receipt, and Grace compared her signature to the one on the back of the credit card. They matched perfectly, and Grace was certain everything was fine. She wanted to keep the long line moving. So she returned the card to the woman, handed over the shopping bag, and waved good-bye."

"I've got a bad feeling about this," said Woodrow.

Rosie nodded. "About an hour later, Tori called Grace into the office at the back of the store. Tori was angry. 'I told you to watch that customer closely,' she said. 'And you let her steal almost five hundred dollars worth of merchandise from us.'

"'You saw the woman use *a* credit card,' said Tori. 'It just happened to be a *stolen* credit card.'

"Grace got really frustrated. 'But I checked the signature,' she answered. 'It matched the name on the card.'

"Tori sighed. 'If you checked the woman's signature against the name on the card, you should have noticed a problem immediately,' she said."

"What was the problem?" asked Woodrow.

The group was quiet for a few minutes. "Maybe the signature was a really silly name," said Sylvester. "Like Minnie Mouse or something like that."

Rosie shook her head. "It was a real name belonging to a real person. *But what kind of name should have instantly clued my sister in that she was being scammed by this woman?*"

Viola gasped. "Was it a man's name on the card?"

"Yes," said Rosie. "The card belonged to a man named John Whiting. The woman had stolen Mr. Whiting's wallet that afternoon and had been on a shopping spree ever since, hoping people wouldn't look too closely at the first name on the card. Mr. Whiting alerted the authorities as soon as he realized his card was missing. My sister just happened to be one of the unlucky ones who got taken in by the woman's charm."

"Ugh," said Sylvester. "That makes me so angry!"

"I have a question," said Woodrow. "Grace said the signature matched the one on the card. How is that possible?"

"Maybe she practiced copying his handwriting before using it," Sylvester suggested.

"Wouldn't that have taken a lot of work?" said Viola. "Probably more than just a few minutes . . . and it sounds like she didn't have a lot of time."

"That's a really good question, Woodrow," said Rosie. *"How did the woman manage to forge Mr. Whiting's handwriting on the credit slips so perfectly?"*

"She must not have forged it at all," said Sylvester, as the idea slowly came to him.

"What do you mean?" Woodrow asked.

"I've noticed my mom ring up customers at our diner. Sometimes people don't sign the back of their credit card."

"Yes!" said Viola. "This John Whiting guy must have left his card blank. After the woman stole it, she simply signed his name for him there. That way, the signatures on the card and the credit slip would match."

"Poor Grace," said Sylvester. "Did she get fired?"

Rosie shook her head. "Tori scolded her for not being more careful. But since the police caught the woman less than an hour later, the store recovered the merchandise and Mr. Whiting got his money back. Still, my sister was so embarrassed, she wanted to quit. But my parents told her these things happen all the time and talked her out of making a hasty decision."

"Those things *do* happen all the time," said Woodrow. "When I visited my dad in New York City last weekend, we had our own experience with a thief."

5

THE JUICY LIE
(A ? MYSTERY)

"Last Saturday, my dad met me at Grand Central Station as usual," said Woodrow. "But this time, he surprised me with tickets to go see a Broadway show."

"Really?" said Viola. "I didn't picture you being into stuff like that."

"Well, it was a really cool show," said Woodrow, blushing. "The cast was funny and the story was twisted. Plus, I liked the music."

"So I guess you *are* into stuff like that," said Sylvester.

"If you mean 'really cool stuff,' I guess I am." He puffed out his chest. "And if you're lucky, maybe I'll invite you next time. A fine cultural experience might do you some good," he said, nudging his friend's shoulder. "Anyway, after the show and a late dinner, Times Square was a little bit quieter than I'm used to. My dad and I were walking up Broadway back to his apartment when this big, burly guy totally knocked into me. I nearly fell over. The plastic bag he'd been carrying slipped out of his hand and fell to the

49

sidewalk. A glass bottle inside the bag shattered. My dad and I paused as the man grunted in annoyance. He immediately scooped up the mess and tossed it in the nearest trash can. We started to walk away when the man called out at us, 'Don't tell me you're not even going to apologize!'

"I could tell my father was biting his tongue, since the man was the one who'd crashed into me. But my dad managed to politely apologize, and we continued to walk away.

"'That's not good enough,' the man called out. 'You owe me another juice.' Not wanting to cause any trouble, my dad said, 'Fine. How much?'

"The guy didn't hesitate. 'Fifty bucks.'"

"Fifty dollars?" said Viola. "What kind of juice was it?"

"That's what I wondered," said Woodrow. "The man explained that he'd just come from his gym. And he looked like it. He had huge muscles. He told us that the juice had been a special shake with protein powder and all sorts of exotic vitamins in it. That's why it cost so much money.

"Not wanting to hand over a wad of money on the street, my dad offered to walk to the man's gym to buy him another one. The guy agreed and then told us that his gym was all the way over on Eleventh Avenue."

"That's practically the Hudson River," said Sylvester.

Woodrow nodded. "My dad started to get nervous. I could tell he didn't want to follow a stranger anywhere. But we were scared that if we just tried to walk away, he'd follow us home. And there were no cops around—believe me, I looked. Because as we stood there, something about the situation felt strange."

"You think?" said Viola.

"It started to stink . . . like a scam. This guy just *happened* to bump into me on a nearly deserted street. He just *happened* to drop the drink he was carrying. It just *happened* to be a really expensive drink that was only available four avenue blocks away. I knew we needed to figure out a way to outwit this guy, to prove that he was lying. Suddenly, it came to me. All I needed was right there on the street with me. ***Do you guys know how I called his bluff?***"

"The broken juice bottle?" asked Rosie.

Woodrow nodded. "Nonchalantly, I wandered over to the trash can where the man had tossed his plastic bag. 'What was the brand of your drink?' I asked. 'Maybe we can find it at a store around here instead.' My dad threw me a look that said I should keep quiet, but it was too late. I'd already pulled a piece of the man's bottle from the bag. The label revealed that the supposedly expensive protein drink was actually an ordinary bottle of apple juice."

"Whoa," said Rosie. "What did he do then?"

"The guy knew he'd been caught. He took a few steps away, mumbled 'never mind,' and took off around the corner.

"My dad made me promise to let him handle that sort of thing from now on. But he did buy me an apple juice on the way home to reward me for my detective work. It cost a lot less than fifty bucks!"

6

A NO LONGER SECRET SOCIETY

Early the next day, Sylvester, Viola, Woodrow, and Rosie were called to Principal Dzielski's office. Together, they sat nervously and waited in silence for what felt like too long. Had they done something wrong, they wondered?

Finally, Ms. Dzielski swung the door open and strode into the room. She wore a brown tweed pencil skirt and a white blouse with ruffles running down the front. Her black hair was pulled back into a tight ponytail, which made her usually kind face look severe and a bit older than her fifty years. "Hello there" was all she said. She crossed briskly to her desk and sat down. She folded her hands and leaned forward.

Viola's heart raced. She tried to plan a counterargument in case Ms. Dzielski accused them of misconduct. Sylvester's mouth had gone dry. All he could think about was the water fountain in the hallway just outside the office. Rosie simply sat still. There was no reason to jump to conclusions. Right? And Woodrow thought about the video game he'd been playing the night before, trying to come up with a solution for beating the horde of bad guys who'd kept defeating his character: Razmore, the Drab.

"I understand you four have made a name for yourselves," said Ms. Dzielski at last. She smiled. "Congratulations. I read the article in the *Herald*."

"Thanks," said Viola, tentatively speaking for the entire group.

"I was thinking it might be a fun idea to have you all talk to your peers about your experience. What do you say?"

The four glanced at one another, unsure what to think. Sylvester spoke up. "You mean, like, in the auditorium?"

"Absolutely," said Ms. Dzielski. "It would be inspiring for the other students to hear how you figured out the clues in the clocks."

"But everybody already read about it in the newspaper," said Woodrow. "Why do we have to talk about it even more?"

"Well . . . you don't *have* to." The principal leaned back. She looked at him as if she wanted to peek inside his head. "I thought maybe you'd like to share—"

"I don't really want to," Woodrow interrupted. The rest of the group stared at him in shock. "We're a *secret* society."

"Secret society?" Ms. Dzielski chuckled. "There's nothing secret about you kids anymore."

"We'll think about it, Ms. Dzielski," said Rosie, trying to smooth over Woodrow's rudeness.

The principal stared at them for a moment. "Fair enough," she said. She looked as if she were about to let them go, when, wearing a curious expression, she asked, "How much do you really know about the Timekeepers of Moon Hollow?"

None of the group knew what to say. The question hinted that there was more to the clock clues than what they had learned. Viola was the one to speak up. "We know what we told the newspapers." She blinked, and with a careful, blank tone added, "Why? Do you know something else about them?"

Ms. Dzielski sat up straight. "Me?" She took a deep breath, and something hidden deep inside her seemed to shift. She smiled again. "I just really wish you would consider sharing your story with the rest of the school. This town needs more kids like you."

After the principal dismissed the group, they paused in the quiet hallway. "Is something wrong?" Viola asked Woodrow. "I thought we all agreed it was okay to talk about what we found."

Woodrow crossed his arms. "I guess I just didn't expect people to pay so much attention. Everyone has been staring at me all day long."

"I thought you liked the girls staring at you," said Rosie, raising an eyebrow.

"That's not what I'm talking about. This whole

thing is . . . strange. I liked it better when it was just ours."

"But you didn't feel this way yesterday," Sylvester said.

Woodrow was quiet for a moment. Then he shrugged. "When I got home last night, my mom and her new boyfriend, Bill, were sitting on the couch watching television. Bill started asking me all sorts of questions. About the Timekeepers. About our mystery club. I didn't want to answer him. Then, I realized I didn't want to answer *anyone*."

"I'm sorry," said Viola, feeling especially guilty. "I had no idea this was going to weird you out. I wouldn't have let my mom write about us in the paper."

"What's going to happen when Darlene's interview with us is finally published?" Sylvester asked.

"How about we just forget it for now," Rosie suggested. "We still have our mysteries. Let's focus on those and ignore the rest of it. Okay?"

The group agreed that their mysteries would belong to them and only them, no matter who asked.

7

THE MYSTERY OF THE BROWNIE BANDIT
(A ??? MYSTERY)

By the end of the week, school gossip had begun in full force. Each member of the group was suddenly very popular at lunch. Everyone wanted to sit with them, which was nice at first, but by Friday afternoon, even Viola, who had the gift of gab, was tired of it—especially after the group pact to keep the mysteries to themselves. The four desperately needed a distraction.

After school, the group gathered at the Knox house, sitting on the floor in Woodrow's bedroom. Before Viola had a chance to call the meeting to order, Sylvester began scratching at his ankles. "What's wrong with you?" Woodrow asked.

"I'm not sure," said Sylvester, pulling up the cuff of his jeans. "I've been really itchy lately."

"Whoa," said Rosie, examining a row of red bumps running up Sylvester's leg. "You've been bitten."

"Bitten?" said Woodrow. "By what?"

"I'm not sure," said Rosie. "It doesn't look like a mosquito. And a spider bite would hurt, not itch. Maybe strange insects live in that basement of yours. Have you ever heard of tiger crickets?"

"No . . . ," Sylvester answered slowly. "Do I want to?"

"Of course! I could come over and help you track them down. I'll bring my biology kit to collect samples."

"Uh, great," said Sylvester, trying to put the thought out of his head. He pulled his pant cuff down tightly and squeezed his ankle.

"So what did you want to tell us, Viola?" Woodrow asked.

"My mom was listening to the police scanner yesterday," Viola said, perking up. "I wanted to share her story with you guys to see what you thought."

"Go ahead," said Sylvester. "Shoot."

"You guys know Naomi's Bakery on Main Street, right?" said Viola.

"I love their chocolate chip cookies," said Rosie, her eyes lighting up.

"Their brownies are even better," said Sylvester, still tugging at his pant cuff. "In fact, that's where my parents buy their baked goods for the diner."

"Those brownies are award-winning," Woodrow chimed in, his eyes glassy as he pictured them. "They're gooey and fluffy at the same time, with an almost-crisp top. I wish we had some right now."

"We sell out every day," Sylvester continued. "And my mom says that Naomi Klipkin is really protective of her recipes. Supposedly her grandmother left them to her and only her. She doesn't share them with anyone. In fact, she told my mom that she keeps her recipe-card box locked up in a safe at the bakery."

Viola sighed. "It's interesting that you mention that, because according to my mom, someone has broken into her store several times this week."

"Oh no," said Rosie. "That's terrible. Did they steal a lot of money?"

"Not money," said Viola. "Brownies!"

"Someone has been stealing the *brownies* from Naomi's Bakery?" Woodrow asked, baffled. "What is wrong with people?"

Sylvester laughed. "The brownies are that good!"

Viola continued. "Three mornings this week, Naomi came into work and found that the trays of brownies she'd baked late the night before were empty. There was no sign of forced entry. The bandit had left only crumbs.

"Naomi's sister, Sadie, who works at the bakery, lives across the street. She has a perfect view of the entrance. On the third morning, Sadie claimed that she saw someone coming out of the front door carrying a large parcel. She presumed it was a box filled with brownies."

"Did she say who the person was?" said Woodrow.

"Sadie claimed it was Vernon Haynes, the owner of the only other bakery in town. His store, Moon Hollow Sweets, is over on Spencer Street."

"A bakery rivalry!" Sylvester proclaimed. "Of course!"

"Sadie accused Vernon of stealing Naomi's goods so that he could analyze them and acquire the recipe to drive her out of business," said Viola.

"That's quite an accusation," said Rosie.

"So what did Vernon have to say for himself?" Woodrow asked.

"He told police that anyone with half a brain would know that Sadie was lying," said Viola.

"But how?" asked Sylvester.

Rosie spoke up. "If Vernon wanted to get his hands on Naomi's brownies, he wouldn't have had to steal them once, let alone three times in a week. All he'd have to do is *buy* some."

"Exactly," said Viola. "And the police weren't buying Sadie's story either. They believed she was jealous of Naomi's business and was trying to sabotage it."

***"But what proof did they have?"* asked Woodrow.**

"Sadie claimed she saw Vernon coming out of the store carrying the parcel of brownies," said Rosie. "But if he'd done that, he would have left some sort of evidence of breaking in, right? Since the brownies disappeared without any signs of forced entry, they knew the thief had access to the store."

"Sadie works there, so she must have a key," said Sylvester. "Since she lives across the street, she could get in and out late at night without anyone noticing."

"Yeah," said Woodrow, "but I still don't understand why she would do it. Stealing the award-winning brownies from her sister isn't necessarily going to put Naomi out of business, right?"

"True," said Viola. "But stealing the brownies might have provided a distraction from what Sadie really wanted to get her hands on. *Can you guess what it was?*"

"The recipes!" shouted Rosie.

"You got it," said Viola. "After searching Sadie's apartment, the police found the recipe box, which she had taken from the bakery's safe. In all the confusion with the missing brownies, no one thought to look for what else might have been missing."

"She'd stolen the recipes *and* the brownies?" Sylvester said, almost impressed.

"Faced with overwhelming evidence of her guilt, Sadie confessed," said Viola. "She admitted she was sick of her sister getting praise for something that their grandmother had invented. She claimed that her grandmother had left those recipes to the both of them, and that Naomi had no right to lock them away from her. She figured that if she blamed Vernon Haynes for stealing the brownies, then when Naomi eventually discovered that her recipe box was missing too, Vernon would look responsible for all of it. By then it would be too late. She'd planned on distributing the recipes online."

"Wow," said Sylvester. "I bet Naomi had no idea she had a complete stranger working with her."

"And her own sister too," Rosie added.

"Yeah, just awful," said Woodrow. "That story made me hungry. . . . Hey, who wants a snack?"

8

THE PINE TREE ABDUCTIONS
(A ??? MYSTERY)

A few minutes later, the smell of popcorn filled the kitchen where the group now gathered. Woodrow opened the microwave's door moments before the kernels inside the bag might have burned. He was a pro at this.

"My mom told me a story last night," said Woodrow, bringing the popcorn to the kitchen table. "She thought this would be a good one to share with you guys. She said that at work recently, she's been investigating this one particular area of the park that is filled with pine trees. Over the past month, someone has been cutting them down."

"That's horrible!" said Rosie through a mouthful of kernels.

"I know. And totally illegal. She said that when a colleague was patrolling an area up in the hills, he noticed that there were freshly cut stumps. The trees themselves were missing. Stolen. The next time my mom and her colleague went up to the area, the thieves had taken even more."

"How would someone do that?" asked Sylvester. "Steal a tree."

"With a big truck," Viola suggested.

"But it's easy enough to buy lumber," said Rosie. "Why steal it?"

"I guess it can get expensive if you need a lot of it," said Viola. "I mean, why do people *usually* steal things?"

"Because they can't afford it?" asked Sylvester.

"That's what my mom figured," said Woodrow. "So she and her coworkers put their heads together to think about what someone might do with large tree trunks."

"You can chop them up!" said Sylvester. "Turn them into boards to build houses."

"Sure," said Woodrow. "That was one of their theories. They checked all the local construction sites. None of them were using the type of pine that had been stolen from the park."

"What about for firewood?" suggested Rosie.

"That would be a LOT of firewood," said Woodrow.

"Mulch?" Viola suggested. "People use wood chips in their yards for landscaping decoration."

Woodrow nodded. "They thought of that too. All the local landscapers checked out as well. They had receipts and could prove where they got their supplies from. Eventually, my mom and

65

her coworkers began to wonder if the thieves might have come in from out of town."

Viola shook her head. "I don't think so. Whoever it was must be from Moon Hollow."

"Why do you think that?" asked Woodrow.

"You mentioned that the cuttings have occurred several times. If someone was coming in from outside this area to steal these trees, they would have to come back over and over. Someone would have recognized strange trucks passing through Moon Hollow, even if it was at night, don't you think?"

"But even if it's someone from town," said Sylvester, "wouldn't we all notice a truck with a huge pine tree tied to its bed?"

"Not if it was a type of truck we're used to seeing," said Viola. The group looked at her funny, waiting for her to continue.

"I don't know about the rest of you," said Rosie, "but I don't remember ever seeing something like that."

"I do." Viola shrugged. "I can think of one company around here that might be able to pass unnoticed even while carrying a pine tree. *Can you?*"

"The telephone company!" shouted Sylvester.

Woodrow and Viola nodded together.

"They're using the trees as utility poles?" said Rosie. "How scandalous."

"That's exactly who my mom and her coworkers approached next," said Woodrow. "You know those roads the town is building out near the highway? The new area needed telephone poles, and the phone company hired a local firm to help set them up. When the park rangers approached the foreman, asking where the firm's wood came from, he couldn't provide invoices. My mom immediately thought they had their culprit in the bag."

"She *thought* so?" said Sylvester.

"Like we always say, if you're going to accuse someone, you need undeniable proof."

"So the firm got off the hook?" said Rosie, disappointed.

"Hardly," said Woodrow, with a smirk. "My mom told them that she would need to examine their supply of wood."

"And that worked?" said Rosie.

"It sure did."

"Still . . . what was your mom's proof?" asked Sylvester. ***"How was she sure the fresh-cut wood that she examined came from the trees in the park?"***

"I know," said Rosie. "Tree rings!"

"Yup," said Woodrow. "My mom had taken snapshots of the tree stumps from the park. She was able to compare those pictures to the cross-section of inner rings from the phone poles on the firm's lot. The rings matched up like fingerprints."

"So your *mom* actually caught these guys," said Viola, a bit awestruck.

"They're going to be slapped with some hefty fines. I guess cutting down the park trees didn't actually help them cut costs."

"That is *so* cool," said Rosie.

"Yeah," said Woodrow. "I guess my mom can be pretty awesome when she feels like it."

9

THE FIGURE AT THE FOUR CORNERS

Later, after his friends went home, after his mother had come into his bedroom and said good night, Woodrow sat in bed feeling odd. He wondered if the feeling was from all the stories he and his friends had been sharing. Why did people treat one another this way? Did these bizarre things happen everywhere? Had the Question Marks raised so many questions about their town simply because they'd been looking for them? Or was there something wrong with Moon Hollow?

Take Bill for instance—Woodrow's constant question mark. Every time the man visited, he tried to one-up himself with kindness. Earlier that week, Bill had given Woodrow a pen that read *One Cent Savings and Trust*—the bank where he worked. What kind of person would want to *save* only one cent? Why would you *trust* someone like that? And what kind of a lame gift was a pen, anyway?

A noise came from outside. *Chck!* Woodrow held still. It came again—a jarring, scraping sound in the backyard. *Chck! Chck!* He leaned toward his window and pulled back the curtain.

To his surprise, he found someone standing on the lawn—right at the Four Corners.

It was difficult to make out any details. In the darkness, Woodrow couldn't tell if the figure was tall or short, fat or thin, but he noticed that he or she was holding what looked like a long stick.

Chck! The sound came again, and Woodrow realized that what the person held was a shovel. The figure was digging up the Four Corners!

Woodrow threw his covers off and leapt from his mattress. Dressed in flannel pajamas, he pulled open his door and raced down the hall. Knocking on his mother's door, he called, "Mom! Quick! There's an intruder!"

From inside her bedroom, Mrs. Knox groggily answered, "What's the matter?" Woodrow took that as his cue to enter. He found her struggling to rise from her bed, obviously woken from a deep sleep. She rubbed her eyes. Taking her hand, he led her to her bedroom window, which also looked out on the backyard.

"Look," he said, drawing up the shades. But now, a hard yellow light shone from the Harts' back stoop, reaching nearly across the now empty yard. "Oh no," Woodrow moaned. "Whoever was there must have triggered the Harts' motion sensor."

"What am I supposed to be looking at?" his mother asked.

"There was someone out there."

"We do have neighbors."

"Someone was digging in the backyard!"

Mrs. Knox groaned. "There are more important things to worry about in this world than someone who likes to garden by moonlight." She took Woodrow's hand and paraded him back to the hallway. "Good night," she said. "Again."

But Woodrow couldn't sleep. Instead, he went downstairs to the computer and sent out a very important e-mail.

The group met at the Four Corners the next morning just as Woodrow had requested. And just as he had expected, they found a fresh hole in the ground yawning up at them. In his e-mail, he'd asked that everyone check with their families to rule them out as possible suspects. No one in any of the four houses admitted to being out there the night before.

"You're sure you don't know what the person looked like?" Viola asked, holding her pen over a blank page in her notebook.

"Other than having two arms and two legs, well . . . no."

Rosie knelt down to examine the hole. "Not very wide or deep. Whoever did this must have been interrupted fairly quickly."

"I told you," said Woodrow, pointing at the Hart house's back door. "The light."

"Are there any other clues worth noting?" Sylvester asked, peering at the frostbitten lawn. "Footprints?"

"I don't see anything," said Viola, flipping her notebook shut and glancing around the yard.

"What could the person possibly have been up to?" said Woodrow. "Why here?"

The group watched one another in silence, afraid to say what they were all thinking. In the *Herald* interview, Viola had mentioned that their mystery club usually gathered behind their houses, where their yards met in an invisible X. And everyone knows that X always marks the spot. The hole in the ground was proof that someone was searching for something the group might have hidden. Two questions floated unspoken in the icy air a few feet above the Four Corners: What had the figure been looking for . . . and where would he or she find it?

1θ

THE CASE OF THE FOUR-LEAF CLOVER
(A ??? MYSTERY)

The next week, Thanksgiving came to Moon Hollow. That Thursday morning, Viola's parents scrambled to pack the car with cookies, breads, and one still-warm pie to take to Viola's uncle's house outside of Philadelphia. Next door, Mr. and Mrs. Smithers extended the dining room table as far as possible in preparation for the coming swarm of relatives. In the house to their rear, Woodrow put on a shirt and tie and his mother wore a festive dress to meet Bill's family. And Sylvester was stuck at home with his grandmother and baby sister, because his parents insisted on opening the diner in case anyone in town didn't have family with whom to share the holiday.

One day later, turkeys had been devoured, pie plates licked clean, dishes stacked in sinks, and leftovers packaged and frozen. That afternoon, Viola invited her friends over for pecan pie and hot mulled cider. They sat in the kitchen as Viola's parents watched a movie in the den.

"Who's first?" Viola asked, before shoving a forkful of caramel and crust into her mouth.

"I've got one," said Sylvester. "It happened at school on Wednesday, before we got out early for the holiday. Do you guys know Wendy Nichols?"

"How could we not?" said Woodrow. "She's one of the weirdest girls in the sixth grade." Receiving scowls from both Rosie and Viola, he tried to modify his tune. "I mean . . . she's cool too. Really sweet." But he failed. "Aw, c'mon, she's just *weird!*"

"I haven't met her," said Viola. "How's she weird?"

"Sometimes she wears her T-shirts backward during gym glass," said Sylvester. "And she dyed her hair *gray* last year."

"I thought it was sort of cool looking," said Rosie. "But *my* mom would never let me do something like that."

"My parents would kill me," Viola agreed.

"Well, I think she's funny," said Sylvester. "We're friends. She always asks me to do coin tricks for her between classes. And this week, when we were standing in the hall after first period, she said she had a secret to share. In her bag, she said, was something magic."

"What was it?" the other three asked at the exact same time.

"A four-leaf clover. She'd pressed it between

two pieces of clear plastic tape. She said that according to this old legend, it's good luck to give away a four-leaf clover. The legend says that she'll always find another. Wendy told me she's given away at least *seven* of them."

"Wow," said Viola. "I've got to try it sometime."

"Yeah," said Rosie, "but the trick is to find one in the first place. They're really rare, right?"

"That's why they're considered so lucky," said Woodrow.

"Wendy wasn't so lucky when she showed the clover to me in the hall on Wednesday morning," said Sylvester. "Our old friend, Mickey Molynew, was watching."

"That goon?" said Viola.

"Don't tell me," said Rosie. "He stole it from her?"

Sylvester shrugged. "Wendy mentioned to me after the next period that the lucky clover was missing from her backpack."

"She'd stored it in her locker?" Viola asked.

"No, she'd taken the backpack with her to class," said Sylvester. "When I asked if she thought she might have dropped the clover along the way, she said she was certain she'd tucked it into the front pocket of her bag like she always does. I asked if she noticed anyone suspicious poking around, and she told me who sits right behind her."

"Hmm...I wonder," said Woodrow with a sarcastic smile.

"We put two and two together and realized that Mickey must have overheard her telling me about the lucky clover. He must have wanted it for himself."

"If she lost the clover," said Rosie, "how lucky can it really be?"

Sylvester chuckled. "Funny you mention it, because right then Wendy said that we often have to make our own luck. She was determined to get the clover back from Mickey, and I was willing to help. But we couldn't accuse him of stealing it. He would have denied taking it until the sun set. So we decided we'd have to trick Mickey into revealing where he was keeping it."

"But how?" asked Rosie.

Viola leaned forward. "Can I guess?"

"Go ahead," said Sylvester.

"Wendy needed to act as if she still had the clover," said Viola. "Or had it back again. If she showed off another four-leaf clover while Mickey was nearby, he might think she'd stolen it back from him. He'd be tempted to double-check his own hiding place—and you could nab him."

Sylvester lit up. "That's exactly the plan Wendy came up with to trick Mickey into giving himself away. But we had one very big problem."

"What was the problem?" asked Woodrow.

"They had to find another four-leaf clover," said Rosie.

"Right," Sylvester continued. "And we needed this to happen before the end of the day. If we were too late, Mickey might take the clover home with him, or even toss it away. And if that happened, we wouldn't be able to catch him in the act of double-checking on it."

"But how did you expect to find another one so quickly?" Rosie asked.

Sylvester shrugged. "We went outside during gym class and searched the field. Even though it's late in the season, there was still plenty of clover. Unfortunately, we couldn't uncover any with four leaves."

"So then Wendy's plan didn't work?" asked Viola.

"I'm not saying that." Sylvester smiled mysteriously. "We just had to be . . . let's say . . . a little creative."

"Wait a second," said Woodrow. *"If you didn't find what you were looking for, how did you pull off your plan?"*

"I have an idea," said Rosie. "You didn't *find* another four-leaf clover. You *made* one instead!"

Sylvester nodded. "Wendy picked two perfectly shaped three-leaf clovers. She brought them back inside and asked our gym teacher for two pieces of clear tape. Pulling one leaf from one stem, she added the leaf to the other three-leafed stem. Then, she pressed the sticky sides of the tape together, trapping the fake four-leaf clover inside. It looked exactly like the one she'd lost."

"Voilà!" said Viola. "Brilliant."

"At the end of the day, we waited by Wendy's locker for Mickey to come by. When he showed up, Wendy pulled out the fake clover. Speaking really loudly, we mentioned how lucky we were to have found the clover in the hallway. Mickey heard us. Out of the corner of my eye, I watched him flinch in confusion. He immediately reached into his locker and pulled out a thick textbook. As he flipped through the pages, something fell out of the book. The stolen clover! We watched it flutter to the ground. Then Wendy placed her sneaker over it, bent down, and picked it up.

"Mickey turned bright red, knowing he'd been caught. And Wendy ignored him completely. She simply handed me the real four-leaf clover and said, 'Thanks for your help.'"

"Really?" said Rosie. "She gave it to you?"

Sylvester nodded slyly. "Of course," he said. "I'm keeping it safe at my house. Wendy knew she'd find another one. She always does."

Woodrow leaned across the table and slapped Sylvester's shoulder. "So you finally found yourself a girlfriend? Your luck has certainly changed."

Sylvester turned so red, he looked like he might explode. "She's not my girlfriend," he insisted. "She just wanted to bring me luck!"

"And I'm telling you that it worked!" said Woodrow.

"Okay, then," said Rosie, raising her voice. "Speaking of girlfriends, my brother Stephen told us a story at Thanksgiving dinner yesterday. Wait until you hear *this*."

11
THE SCHOOL DANCE DRAMA
(A ?? MYSTERY)

"Last Friday night was the Freshman-Sophomore Dance at Moon Hollow High," said Rosie. "Stephen went with a friend of his, a girl named Audrey Heckler."

"Wait a second," said Viola. "Isn't Stephen dating Eva what's-her-name?"

"Eva Bentley," said Rosie. "But Audrey asked Stephen to accompany her at the very beginning of the school year, before Stephen and Eva started going out. Audrey and Stephen have been friends forever. My brother didn't think it was right to change his mind and cancel on his friend."

"Was Eva okay with that?" asked Woodrow.

"She said that she didn't have a problem with it," said Rosie, "even though her best friends, Debbie and Olive, who were in charge of the dance decorations, gave her a hard time. They said Eva shouldn't stand for it—that Stephen was being a bad boyfriend. In fact, they were mean to Audrey too, calling her all kinds of names in the locker room the week before the dance."

"Girls," said Sylvester with a sigh.

"Boys can be just as mean," said Viola, offended.

"Anyway," Rosie continued, "Eva told Stephen not to worry about it, that she hated going to dances in the first place. She said she was going to stay home and catch up on some reading she had to do for English class, the one subject that's been giving her trouble this year.

"Audrey lives up in the hills outside of town, and on Friday night, my dad drove my brother to pick her up. He dropped them off at the high school. When they walked through the doors to the gym, there was a huge commotion. Someone had torn down all of Debbie and Olive's decorations. There were crumpled streamers everywhere, and worst of all, the giant papier-mâché turkey they'd built was missing its head!"

"That's horrible!" said Viola.

"While Debbie and Olive stood beside their project, crying about how much time they'd spent putting it together, Stephen noticed that pieces of paper streamers were scattered on the floor. The streamers led out of the gym and down the hallway. He asked Audrey to come with him to see where they ended up. Debbie and Olive pulled it together enough to tag along. One of the chaperones, a math teacher named Mr. Swenk, joined them too. Together, they all followed the trail of destruction up into the sophomore hallway. The decorations stopped in front of one locker, which was open a crack. Audrey gasped. It was her locker. When she opened the door, the turkey head rolled out and landed at Debbie's feet. Olive screamed."

"Just like in a horror movie," Sylvester whispered.

"Do you think someone set Audrey up?" said Woodrow.

The group considered that for a moment. "Maybe not," said Viola, biting the end of her pen. "I mean, Audrey certainly had a reason to want to get back at Debbie and Olive. Those girls were really terrible to her. Right? Did Stephen think Audrey was responsible?" Rosie shook her head. "Why not?"

"Besides the fact that they've been close friends since kindergarten?" Rosie said. "If Audrey had wanted to get back at Debbie and Olive, would she really have been so obvious about it? Leaving a trail of streamers leading directly to her own locker?"

Viola sighed, frustrated. "I don't know."

"Also, Audrey lives really far away from the school," Rosie added. "My dad had picked her up from her house and brought her and Stephen directly to the dance. Unless she had help, it would have been almost impossible for Audrey to destroy the decorations after classes ended, run home, and get ready for the dance. She wouldn't have had time."

"*Almost* impossible isn't the same as impossible," said Woodrow.

"Okay, then," said Viola. "Let's say Audrey wasn't the one who ruined the decorations. *Who else could have done it?*"

"I think the most obvious suspects are Debbie and Olive," said Sylvester. "We already know that they had a problem with Audrey. They were mean to her in the locker room the week before the dance. Maybe they wanted to get her in trouble."

"Yeah," said Woodrow. "If they were the ones who were setting up the decorations after school, they would have still been there before the dance. They would have had time to tear everything down, to rip the head off the giant turkey, and to somehow get it inside Audrey's locker."

"That's exactly what my brother and Audrey thought," said Rosie. "In fact, when Mr. Swenk, the math teacher chaperone, began to scold Audrey, Stephen accused Debbie and Olive right there of sabotaging the dance decorations themselves. Since there really was no solid proof of who was guilty, Mr. Swenk kicked them all out of the dance. My dad had to go pick up my brother and Audrey and take them home."

"Oh man," said Sylvester. "That's pretty bad."

"Stephen was really upset. He called Eva's house to get her thoughts on the matter, but Eva's mom said she'd gone to the library to study. My brother never got a chance to talk to her that night.

"They talked the next day, and Stephen told Eva everything that had happened at the dance. She had already heard most of it from Debbie and Olive, who were still insisting that Audrey was the guilty one. Eva said now she was *really* glad she'd skipped the dance. She'd been able to memorize all the theorems and proofs that had been stumping her in class, and she missed all of the drama too.

"At school on Monday, there was lots of tension in hallways. The rumor mill was running. People kept giving Audrey dirty looks. But my brother said Audrey kept her head held high.

"Stephen was walking to English class to meet up with Eva when he passed the spot where the turkey head had rolled across the floor to land at Debbie and Olive's feet. He said he was instantly struck by a memory from the previous Friday. And he realized he knew for certain who the vandal was. **Can you guys think of what Stephen remembered?"**

"Oh my gosh," said Sylvester, as the answer came to him. "No way!" The group looked at him and waited, but he was dumbstruck.

"Are you going to tell us or not?" prodded Woodrow.

Sylvester nodded. "Stephen was meeting Eva at their English class . . . supposedly the one class Eva said she was having trouble with this year. English class was the reason she decided to stay home from the dance."

"So?" said Woodrow.

"When Stephen asked her about her Friday night, she told him she was at the library working on the theorems and proofs that she'd been struggling with. That doesn't sound like English class to me. So which subject was giving her problems? Math or English?"

"Or neither," said Viola. "She lied! And the fact that she wasn't at home on Friday night when Stephen called her means that she doesn't really have an alibi. She could have gone back to the school before the dance and destroyed the decorations herself."

"*She* was the one who wanted to get Audrey in trouble!" said Woodrow.

Rosie nodded. "That's exactly what my brother suspected. He asked her again about which subject she'd been reviewing at the library. Eva looked at him funny. She knew he realized something was off, and she immediately began making excuses for what she'd done."

"Jealousy can turn people crazy, I guess," said Woodrow.

Rosie shrugged. "Needless to say, Stephen and Eva are no longer seeing each other. In fact, he's trying to figure out a way to tell Audrey exactly what happened. He knows she wasn't the one who tore the head off the papier-mâché turkey . . . but he doesn't want her to tear into anyone else either."

12

THE HAIR-RAISING HAUNT
(A ? MYSTERY)

"That was a really good one, Rosie," said Viola. "I hope everything works out for Stephen and Audrey."

"Me too," said Rosie. "I've always liked her."

"Does anyone want more pie?" Viola asked. Woodrow and Sylvester each raised a hand. Viola nodded at the refrigerator. "Help yourself," she said, then smiled at Rosie, who chuckled. The boys got up from the table, bringing their plates with them. "I've got a mystery for you. This one comes from my mom's brother, my uncle Randall, who we visited yesterday down near Philadelphia.

"I love my uncle. He's really fun and kind of kooky. After spending most of his life in the city, Uncle Randall recently decided to move to an old Victorian house in a nearby suburb. He invited my family not only for Thanksgiving but also for a housewarming party. I think everyone was willing to travel because they were all so curious about his grand new home.

"When we pulled up, I couldn't believe what I was seeing. It was everything I had hoped for him—a great big blue dollhouse with a wrap-around front porch and a huge turret along the side that poked at the sky like a rocket."

"Cool!" said Sylvester. "Did it look haunted?"

"Maybe you shouldn't bring up ghosts in front of Viola," said Woodrow.

Viola laughed, glancing around the dining room, as if a ghost might have been watching them. "You know we haven't had troubles in *this* house since last month. Unfortunately for my uncle, his troubles were only beginning."

Sylvester's mouth dropped open. "You mean—"

"'The new house has a ghost,'" said Viola, nodding. "That's what Uncle Randall told everyone after he carved the turkey."

"Just like that?" asked Rosie. "So casually?"

"He was basically relaying rumors from the previous owners," Viola continued. "The family who lived there before him said that the attic was haunted by the ghost of a little girl who would pull your hair. I don't think Uncle Randall had experienced the sensation himself." Viola breathed deeply. The group leaned forward. "After dinner, my cousins were excited to meet the ghost for themselves. My parents stayed downstairs to help clean up, while Uncle Randall grabbed a flashlight and showed us the way upstairs. Having experienced this type of thing before, I trailed behind, carrying my notebook in

91

case I happened to see anything out of the ordinary. In the upstairs hallway, my cousin Rita located the door that led to the attic. She swung it open to reveal a rickety staircase. One at a time, my cousins went up into the darkness.

"There was no light switch or bulb. Uncle Randall lent his flashlight to Rita, who shined it all over the place. By the brief swipes of light, I was able to take a few notes about what I saw. The roof came down at sharp angles all the way to the creaky wooden floor. Dangling from the rafters, I saw some long thin strands of cobweb. The stuff looked eerie, almost alive. In one corner of the room, there was an old steamer trunk. And that was all; the rest of the room was empty."

"What was in the trunk?" said Sylvester.

"That was what my cousin Rita asked," Viola answered. "Uncle Randall said he had no idea. This was the first time he'd really been up there. 'Let's find out,' Rita said, leading the group forward. I stayed near the top of the stairs, where I had a view of the entire attic. Rita handed the light to her brother, Jared, then leaned down and fiddled with the box's latch. Everyone held their breath as she slowly lifted the top. When she peered inside, she gasped. Turning to face us, she wore a look of horror."

"What was it?" said Sylvester. "What was inside?"

"It was empty!" said Viola. "Rita slowly smiled and raised her hands as if to say, 'Oh well,' when suddenly my other cousin, Hazel, who was standing near the wall, started screaming. This threw everyone else into a panic. Jared swung the flashlight violently around, and I realized that my cousins were all racing toward me. I turned and ran down the stairs. Everyone came spilling from the door behind me, wide-eyed and out of breath. 'What happened?' Rita shouted.

"'Someone touched me,' Hazel squeaked. She said it felt exactly like fingers stroking her hair.

"'Then the story is true!' said Rita. 'The old owners were right. There *is* a ghost in the attic!' I watched my uncle turn green. I could tell he wasn't prepared for this. I decided to put a stop to it before Rita's drama got out of hand.

"'No one pulled anyone's hair,' I said, raising my voice so they all could hear me. 'There's a logical explanation for what Hazel experienced in the attic.'"

"It must have been one of the other cousins playing a trick," said Woodrow. "Any of them could have done it."

"But Viola said that Hazel was backed up near the attic's wall," said Rosie. "She would have noticed if someone else was standing near her."

"So, if it wasn't a trick," said Viola, "what spooked Hazel?"

93

"The cobwebs?" Rosie suggested.

"Hmm," said Viola, satisfied.

Rosie continued. "If the webs were hanging from the rafters like you noticed, it's possible that Hazel got too close, and a few strands of her hair got caught. When she moved, she felt a sensation like someone was pulling at her. Since the webs can be nearly invisible, it would have seemed like a paranormal experience."

"Exactly what I told my family," said Viola. "Perfectly rational."

"That's you, all right," said Woodrow. "A great detective even in the scariest of circumstances."

"Well, thanks," Viola answered. "But my cousins didn't think so."

"What do you mean?" Sylvester asked.

"Rita insisted that there was no way cobwebs could feel like that," Viola said, almost sadly. "I figured I could bring her back upstairs and ask her to stand near the sloping walls, but I decided not to force the issue. Some people want to believe what they want to believe.

"But just before my family said our good-byes, Uncle Randall pulled me aside. Despite what my other cousins thought, he thanked me for putting his mind at ease. He said, for a brief moment, he worried that the house really *was* haunted.

"I just smiled and told him I knew the feeling."

13

THE INTRUDER IN THE BASEMENT

Maybe it was all the talk of ghosts, but when Sylvester came home that evening, his skin felt tingly. It didn't help that when he opened the basement door, he found a light shining at the bottom of the stairs. He didn't remember leaving it on.

A long shadow stretched across the floor. He grabbed at the banister. Steadying his voice, he called out, "Hello?"

A rustling noise echoed up at him. "Just a moment!" came Hal-muh-ni's frantic voice.

"What are you doing down there?" Sylvester stepped on the top stair. It creaked.

"Don't come down!"

"Why not?" Sylvester took another step.

"I . . . I have a gift for you." Hal-muh-ni appeared at the bottom of the stairs, wearing a weird smile. She also wore a ratty old nightgown and bright red silk slippers. She held her hands behind her back.

"A gift?" Sylvester said. "You didn't have to get me anything."

"Come," said his grandmother. He edged down the stairs to meet her. She whipped her hands forward, holding out several crumpled twenty-dollar bills. Sylvester was speechless. "I was going to leave this under your pillow, but you caught me. So naughty."

Sylvester wasn't sure if she was referring to him or to herself. "What's it for?"

"I feel bad that I stole your bedroom," she said, forcing the money into his hands. "You can't possibly be comfortable down here."

"It's not that bad," he admitted.

Hal-muh-ni smiled. "You're a good boy, Sylvester. But don't tell your parents. I don't want them mad at me for spoiling you."

"I won't say a word," Sylvester whispered, as his grandmother crept past him and up the stairs. "Thank you so much."

Later, Sylvester sat at his desk thinking of all the ways he could use his grandmother's gift. Eighty dollars was a lot of money. On the paper-bag book cover of his social-studies textbook, he wrote a list of possible purchases. A Super Soaker water blaster for next summer. An upgrade to his Master Magician Magic Box. New headphones for his CD player—or better yet, an iPod.

He was so lost in thought that he didn't notice the soft crunching sound coming from the other end of the basement, just outside the small window high up in the wall.

But maybe it was for the best that he didn't look up . . . or see the shadowy face peering in at him from behind the dirty glass. If he had, he may never have fallen asleep down in that basement again.

From the corner booth of the Main Street Diner, customers had a view of the plaza in front of the Moon Hollow Library, where one of Mr. Clintock's clocks stood.

On Sunday night, Sylvester, Woodrow, Viola, and Rosie squeezed onto the curved seat and waited for Mr. Cho to bring them their order of french fries. The sun had been down for nearly an hour, and it had been the coldest day yet since fall had begun. Still, the Question Marks had stories to tell and this was as good a place as any—better, even, because of the free food. Viola was busy watching people stroll by the clock, stopping, staring, and pointing.

"Something wrong?" Rosie asked.

It took Viola several seconds to realize that Rosie was talking to her. She turned back toward her friends. "Sorry. I just can't stop thinking about what happened with those clocks. I mean . . . they're just clocks. You would think we've discovered the cure for some horrible disease instead of an old secret society that nobody even cared about a few weeks ago. Don't get me wrong. I'm still really excited about it all. It's just . . . things have gotten—"

"Freaky?" Woodrow suggested.

"Yeah," said Rosie. "I ran into Principal Dzielski in the grocery store with my mom yesterday. Can you believe she asked if we'd thought any more about making a presentation?"

"No way," said Sylvester. "What did your mom say?"

"Of course she thought it was a great idea."

Woodrow groaned.

"This time, Ms. Dzielski presented it to me as a way to get our friends to learn about 'community service.' As if the Timekeepers would have wanted us to do that."

Viola blinked. "I never thought about it like that," she said. "The Timekeepers probably *would* have wanted us to do community service. Don't you think?"

"We don't owe anything to the Timekeepers," said Woodrow. "They've all passed away. In fact, I wish we could just forget about them. Bill keeps . . ." He trailed off, as if embarrassed.

No one spoke for a second. Then, Viola quietly prompted, "Bill keeps . . . ?"

"He keeps bringing it up," Woodrow grumbled. "Whenever he comes around, he tells my mom how smart I was to help figure it out. Like he's trying to win me over or something. He even told his own mother about it during Thanksgiving dinner!"

"What's so bad about that?" asked Rosie. "He's just being nice, isn't he?"

Woodrow threw his hands in the air. "Yes! He's nice! Technically. But I don't trust him. I wonder how much he even really likes my mom. It's like he wants something from *me*."

"Maybe you're imagining things," said Rosie. "Don't you think you should give him a chance?"

"I wish I was imagining things," Woodrow said. "But you haven't seen him in action. Maybe when Darlene's article comes out, he can read all about us instead of asking me tons of questions."

Sylvester leaned forward. "I have a mystery to share if that will make you feel better."

"I guess it couldn't hurt," said Woodrow.

A shadow loomed over the booth. "Did someone order fries?" Mr. Cho smiled down at them, placing the plate in the middle of the table.

14

THE BROKEN WINDOW BLUNDER (A ?? MYSTERY)

"My grandmother was telling my mom and me stories about her old house yesterday," said Sylvester. "And I mean her *old* house. It was almost a hundred years old. Before she moved in with us, she lived there for forty years."

"Whoa," said Viola, pouring ketchup on the corner of the plate. "That's a long time."

Sylvester nodded, reaching for a fry. "Behind her house, there was this great big field. When my mom's brother—my uncle—was our age, he and his friends used to play games out there in the summertime. Tag, kickball, baseball. Hal-muh-ni used to watch them from behind the streaky old panes of glass in the kitchen window, leaning out the back door every now and again to offer them drinks or snacks."

"Kind of like *our* yards," said Rosie. "My dad is always watching us."

"Huh," said Sylvester, "I hadn't thought of that. But yeah. Anyway, this one day, my grandmother left my uncle at home to play with his friends while she went out with my mom to run some errands. The boys all decided to get out their bats and gloves. No sooner had my uncle's friend thrown the first pitch, than the ball flew foul and crashed through Hal-muh-ni's kitchen window."

"Of course," said Viola, shaking her head. "Why didn't I see that coming?" Rosie and Woodrow laughed.

"My uncle instantly panicked. He almost ran upstairs and started packing a bag to leave home. But one of his friends, Tommy, examined the damage and assured my uncle that he could help. Tommy's father owned a construction company, and he'd helped fix a few broken windows before. He ran to his father's supply shed and found a new pane of glass the same size and shape as the one from the kitchen window. He got to work while my uncle cleaned up all the broken glass, and they finished with plenty of time to spare. The fit was perfect. My grandmother had no way of knowing there was ever a problem. . . . At least, that's what the guys thought."

"Uh-oh," said Viola, rubbing her hands together. "I have a feeling he's gonna get it!"

"Later that night," Sylvester continued, "my uncle heard a knock at his bedroom door. My grandmother peered in at him. 'Herbert, do you have something you would like to tell me?' she asked in a sweet voice. My uncle didn't know what to do. If he said no, he would be caught in a lie. If he said yes, he'd have to confess. It's the worst kind of question to hear when you're feeling guilty: *Do you have something you would like to tell me?*"

Rosie sat up straight and said in a mock-sweet voice, "Well, Sylvester? Is there?"

They all laughed and grabbed more fries.

"Only the rest of the story, my dear," he said with a wink.

"So what did your uncle do?" asked Woodrow. "Lie or confess?"

"He confessed. She already knew the truth, of course. But she wasn't too upset. She said she was actually impressed with his . . . What did she call it? Resourcefulness."

"But how did she know he'd broken the window?" asked Woodrow.

Sylvester nodded. "And? What do you think?"

"Your grandmother must have found some broken glass or something," said Viola. "Ooh! Maybe she cut herself on it."

Rosie shook her head. "Sylvester said they cleaned it up."

"Sure," said Viola. "But they could have missed some. Or she might have found shards of glass in the garbage."

Sylvester shook his head. "Even if that were true, it wouldn't be enough to lead my grandmother to the truth of what had happened. *Can you guess why that wouldn't prove anything?*"

"If Hal-muh-ni had found broken glass, she couldn't know that it had come from the window," guessed Rosie. "It could have been a drinking glass. Or a jar."

"Right," said Sylvester. "Broken glass wouldn't necessarily mean a broken window, so it had to be a different clue. *What was it?*"

"Oh!" said Viola. "I know. It was the window itself."

"What do you mean?" Woodrow asked.

"Sylvester said that the fit was perfect. And the glass was brand-new. But the house was old, over sixty years old at that point, and the other panes of glass in the window would *not* be perfect."

"Huh," Rosie murmured, realizing where Viola was going.

"Sylvester mentioned that the window was streaky. Probably filled with imperfections. Sylvester's grandmother must have noticed the difference between the old panes and the new one, and realized that the pane had been replaced."

"And why do you replace a windowpane?" Rosie said, already knowing the answer.

"Because the old one was broken," said Woodrow.

"You guys got it," said Sylvester, scooping a huge dollop of ketchup onto the longest fry. "You can tell that one to Bill next time he asks about us." Woodrow pursed his lips, and Sylvester quickly decided to move on. "So . . . who's next?"

15

THE MYSTERY OF THE MISSING MOUTH GEAR (A ? MYSTERY)

"I've got more sibling drama," said Rosie, "if you can believe it."

"I believe it," said Viola. "Your brothers and sisters are always getting into trouble."

Woodrow licked his lips, catching some salt with his tongue. "Rosie's stories make me cherish my only-child-ness."

"No way," said Sylvester. "I've heard you say you wish you had a brother or sister plenty of times."

Woodrow rolled his eyes. "Why would I need a brother to annoy me when I have *you?*"

"For your information," Rosie said, "brothers and sisters do not exist simply to bother each other." She flicked some salt off the table at the boys. "Sometimes they help each other too."

"That's news to me," said Sylvester. "Gwen does nothing but scream lately. If I have to listen to her anymore, I'm gonna scream myself!"

"Listen to this instead," Rosie said, holding up a hand. "My sister Keira has worn a retainer at night ever since she had her braces removed last year. The retainer is this small, gross, clear plastic thing that's supposed to keep her teeth from moving around."

"Yuck," said Viola. "I hope I never have to wear braces."

"Keira says they hurt really bad. Her retainer can hurt too. Every once in a while, she'll wake up in the morning and realize that she's not wearing it. Sometimes she spits the retainer out in the middle of the night. Other times she somehow manages to take the retainer out in her sleep and place it on the nightstand between our beds."

"How lovely for you," Woodrow said.

"Not so much," said Rosie. "I've asked her not to put it there, but there's no reasoning with someone who's basically sleepwalking. And sharing a bedroom, I guess we're bound to argue. We've had some ridiculous ones lately."

"Like what?" asked Viola.

"One had to do with daylight saving time."

"Why would you get in a fight about that?" said Sylvester. "Keira doesn't want to change the clocks?"

"Ever since the time change," Rosie answered, "the light comes through our bedroom window earlier, shining in my face every morning. But Keira's bed is closer to the windowsill, and she likes the sun coming in. She says it helps her wake up. So Keira pulls the curtain open at bedtime, and I've taken to creeping out of bed in the night and shutting it."

"This is a nice story and everything," said Sylvester, "but is there a mystery to solve here?"

"Oh yeah," said Rosie. "I almost forgot that part! Yesterday morning, Keira woke me up, angry at me for shutting the curtain again. She went to open it, but I asked her to keep it shut so I could sleep a little later. She threw back her covers and stormed out of the room. Somehow, I managed to fall back asleep.

"Later, when I was eating breakfast, I heard Keira fussing around upstairs. My mom called me up to our room. Keira had complained to my mom that I had stolen her retainer.

"I saw that Keira had pulled all the sheets and blankets off our beds, but I didn't see my sister's mouth gear anywhere. It wasn't on the floor. It wasn't on her mattress. The light on our nightstand exposed a pile of clean books with no saliva stains on them."

"Yummy," said Sylvester.

"You didn't steal it," Woodrow asked Rosie. "Did you?" He looked like he half expected her to say yes.

"Of course not," said Rosie. "And my mom knew it. Keira got a good scolding, and Mom told her if she wanted to keep her teeth nice and straight, she could buy herself another retainer with her own money."

"That stinks," said Woodrow.

"So, Keira hasn't found it yet?" Viola asked.

"I didn't say that," said Rosie, smiling. "In fact, before bed last night, Keira just happened to come across it in a very obvious place."

"It fell behind the headboard of her bed," said Woodrow.

"No!" said Sylvester. "I bet a mouse stole it. Your sister found it sticking out of a hole in the floor, where it got stuck after the mouse tried to drag it away."

"That's just silly," said Viola. "Rosie said it wasn't on the floor, so the retainer obviously hadn't fallen behind the headboard. And it most definitely wasn't stolen by a mouse."

"Viola's right," said Rosie. *"If it wasn't on the floor, and it wasn't on the mattress, can you guess where Keira's retainer was?"*

The group thought about it for a few minutes. Then Viola smiled. "The curtains."

"Yeah!" said Woodrow.

"Keira's retainer was in the curtains?" said Sylvester.

"No . . . Rosie and Keira have a routine with their curtains," said Viola. "Keira likes them open. Rosie gets out of bed and closes them late at night. Well, yesterday morning, when Keira woke up, Rosie asked her to keep the curtains shut so she could sleep. Later, Keira thought she'd lost her retainer. You guys searched the bedroom, but you never said you opened the curtains again before bedtime."

"Ah," said Sylvester.

"Right," said Rosie. "When Keira got into bed that night, she opened the curtains and found her retainer sitting on the windowsill!"

"She must have put it there the night before while she was half-asleep," said Viola. "Then, when Rosie got up in the middle of the night, she accidentally hid the retainer behind the curtain."

"So then no one stole it," said Woodrow.

"Not even a mouse," Sylvester added with a grin. They all chuckled.

"And the best part," Rosie added, "is that Keira doesn't have to buy herself a new one. I would have felt really guilty about that."

"But it wasn't your fault," said Sylvester.

"I know that," Rosie answered quietly. "But even though Keira and I argue, she's still my sister. And that counts for something. You'll see someday. Gwen won't be a baby forever."

16

THE CASE OF THE CREEPING FINGER
(A ?? MYSTERY)

As Rosie concluded her story, Mr. Cho brought over glasses of water. The group was parched after so much salt and talk. They all gulped noisily.

"I hung out with Kyle Krupnik earlier today," said Woodrow. "We were tossing a ball in his backyard when he told me a crazy story about his next-door neighbors, Mr. and Mrs. Pilson."

"I know them," said Rosie. "They're retired professors. They spend lots of time at the library. Since they're always raising their voices at each other, my mom is constantly asking them to be quiet. She says they have no consideration. I think they're just deaf."

"Deaf or not, they're not very nice people," Woodrow continued. "Last year, we were playing in Kyle's backyard. We accidentally stepped onto their property. Next thing we knew, Mr. Pilson leaned out a window and shouted at us that we were trespassing. He threatened to call the police. Kyle said that a month later, the Pilsons built a tall wooden fence between their property

111

and the Krupniks'. The Pilsons also had a professional gardener plant a whole bunch of bamboo plants for privacy. Since then, the plants have grown really tall, really quickly.

"Even with a privacy fence, Kyle can usually hear them fighting with each other at all hours," said Woodrow. "But when I went over there this morning, it was really quiet. Kyle told me that he hadn't heard them arguing in a while. In fact, he mentioned that for the past few days he's seen Mr. Pilson driving around by himself, which he never does."

"Maybe that's a good thing," said Rosie. "It sounds like they might need some time apart."

"Kyle figured that they might have gotten just that," said Woodrow. "But not in the way you're thinking."

"What do you mean?" asked Viola.

"He thought it was weird that Mrs. Pilson wasn't around. And he wondered if maybe she was . . . gone for good."

The rest of the group turned pale. They finally understood what Woodrow meant.

"Lots of people argue," said Viola. "That doesn't mean they go around 'getting rid' of one another."

"According to Kyle, Mr. Pilson was working in his garden near the fence late yesterday evening. Supposedly, from the street, Kyle noticed that the old man had dug a deep hole."

"To bury his wife in?" said Sylvester, practically shouting. "No way. Not in Moon Hollow."

"I thought the same thing," Woodrow said. "But then Kyle and I crept toward the fence to see if we could get a better idea of what was happening on the other side." He paused, taking another sip of water. "That's when we saw it."

"Saw what?" said Rosie, panic edging in.

"The finger," said Woodrow.

The group was silent for a few seconds. Then Viola whispered, "You found a human finger today and you waited until just now to tell us?"

"Where was it?" Sylvester interrupted. "What did it look like?"

"It looked old and brown and withered, all knobby and filthy." Woodrow licked his lips. The other three kids dropped their jaws in shock. "It was on the Krupniks' side of the fence, opposite Mr. Pilson's hole. It was coming up from the ground, as if trying to claw out of a grave."

"So you called the police?" said Viola.

"We didn't even think to at first," said Woodrow. "Right then, Mr. Pilson came out of his house mumbling and grumbling. He headed right over to the bamboo plants near the fence. We held our breath. He must have sensed that we were there because he started yelling about how 'difficult it was to have privacy anymore.' Kyle and I took off for his house. Once

113

inside, we peeked out the window near the back door to see if Mr. Pilson was coming after us with his shovel.

"In the kitchen, Kyle's mom snuck up behind us and asked what we were doing. We jumped, terrorized. When we had calmed down, Kyle explained that we were certain Mr. Pilson had buried his wife in the bamboo bed, and that Mrs. Pilson had tried to climb under the fence to escape, but didn't make it.

"To our surprise, Mrs. Krupnik started laughing. Hard. She assured us that we'd let our imaginations get the best of us. She was certain that Mr. Pilson had done nothing to his wife. We begged her to call the police, but she refused. *Do you guys have an idea why Mrs. Krupnik was so sure of herself?"*

"The only thing I can think of," said Rosie, "is that maybe Mrs. Krupnik recently saw Mrs. Pilson."

"Exactly," Woodrow answered. "Mrs. Pilson had been away for the past few days. She'd arrived home this morning and greeted Mrs. Krupnik in the driveway, sometime before Kyle had even gotten out of bed."

"Ha," said Sylvester. "Kyle needs to check his sources a little better before accusing anyone of murder again anytime soon."

"You think?" said Woodrow, laughing.

"But what about the finger?" said Viola. "There's still the question of the corpse in the bamboo patch, isn't there?"

"Well," Rosie began, "now that we've ruled out the possibility that the finger was attached to Mrs. Pilson, I think I have another idea about what Kyle and Woodrow found near the fence. It wasn't a dead finger. In fact, I think the object they saw was very much alive."

"Alive?" said Viola, looking squeamish.

"Don't tell me it was a weird snake-lizard thing," said Sylvester.

Rosie smiled but shook her head. "Good guess though. *Anyone else think you know what it was?*"

"I wonder why Mr. Pilson was digging a hole on his side of the fence," said Viola, reasoning through it. "Since he wasn't burying his wife, like Woodrow and Kyle suspected, maybe he was doing something a little more ordinary . . . like gardening."

"Mm-hm," said Rosie, nodding. "Sounds to me like all Mr. Pilson was guilty of was over-zealous landscaping. . . . Well, that and being in a generally foul mood. He didn't realize what he'd gotten himself into by planting bamboo shoots along the fence. I've read that they grow really quickly. Unless you contain them, their roots will spread out far and wide."

Sylvester tapped his chin, "Then the finger you found—"

"Wasn't a finger at all," said Woodrow. "It must have been a root from the bamboo plant invading the Krupniks' yard."

"It's amazing how creepy some plants can appear," said Rosie. "I remember seeing some weird ones at the botanic garden in New York City last summer. They looked like they could have reached out and grabbed us."

"Like this!" Sylvester clutched at Woodrow's arm. Woodrow jumped high enough to bump his knees on the bottom of the table. The water glasses nearly toppled. The four roared with laughter.

17

THE STRANGER IN THE DINER

Mr. Cho called across the restaurant. "Everything okay over there?"

The group immediately settled down. "Sorry, Dad," Sylvester answered.

Mr. Cho nodded then mouthed, "We've got a customer." He slyly pointed at the booth adjacent to theirs before heading into the kitchen. Sylvester turned and noticed someone sitting with his back to them. The man wore a dark flannel dress coat. His broad shoulders accentuated the worn seams of his clothing. His pale scalp was visible underneath his stringy brown hair. He coughed, reached for his coffee mug, and took a sip. Sylvester figured the man had come into the diner during one of their stories.

The man seemed to notice that he was being watched. He glanced over his shoulder at the group. Everyone immediately lowered his or her head, pretending to find the paper placemats on the table the most interesting objects they'd ever seen.

"Excuse me," said the man, his voice a low rumble. He stood and went to their table, his

117

body blocking their view of the kitchen door and of Mr. Cho beyond it. The man wiped his mouth and said, "You kids wouldn't happen to be members of the Question Marks Mystery Club, would you?" Surprised, none of them were able to speak. "Sorry, I couldn't help overhearing your stories. I read about you in the paper."

Viola sat up straight. "Yes, we are the Question Marks." Woodrow pressed his lips and tilted his head at her, silently asking her to quit talking. "We didn't mean to be so noisy. Sorry to bother you."

"Not a bother," said the man, smiling. "It's an honor to meet you all." He stretched out his hand to Viola. As she reluctantly shook it, she noticed dirt underneath his fingernails and around his cuticles. "I'm Phineas Galby. Passing through Moon Hollow on my way to see some family upstate. You kids live in a great little town." He had an accent of some sort. Southern maybe. He stepped back from the table and leaned toward the window, glancing up and down the quiet street. They could now see his entire outfit. An untucked, dark navy button-down shirt. A wrinkled red-and-blue striped tie. The cuffs of his dressy black pants and his leather shoes were muddy.

The clock down the street began to chime.

"Yup, it's a sweet place to live," said Woodrow,

with an air of finality. "It was nice to meet you too. Have fun with your family."

The man, Phineas, turned back to face them. If he was offended by Woodrow's tone, he did not show it. His smile was plastered from cheek to cheek. "Hey," he continued, nodding in the direction of the library around the corner, "is that the clock you kids decoded? The one that helped you find out about those people, the Timekeepers?"

Sylvester nodded. He wished the man would just leave them alone.

"Have you learned anything else about them?" asked Phineas. "Secret societies might have more secrets than the ones you discover on the Internet."

The group all glanced at one another. That was a strange thing for the man to say. Curious, Viola spoke up. "We haven't learned anything else about the Timekeepers. Why do you ask? Do you know anything else about them?"

Phineas's smile flickered for a moment. But just for a moment. He considered Viola's question, and just as he looked like he'd decided to shake his head, he nodded instead. "Some people believe that there's more to the Timekeepers than what was mentioned in your little article," he said.

Woodrow's mouth went dry. He sipped his water, then asked, "Like what?"

Before he had a chance to answer, Phineas

spun around, revealing Mr. Cho. Sylvester's father had tapped the man's large shoulder.

"I hope my son and his friends weren't bothering you," said Mr. Cho, with an edge of suspicion in his voice.

"Your son?" said Phineas, peering back at the group. The smile had disappeared from his face. "Oh. No. No bother at all. I, uh, should be heading out." He pulled his wallet from the inside pocket of his coat and tossed a few crumpled bills onto the table where he'd been sitting. Before anyone could say another word, the man pushed past Mr. Cho and out the door into the night.

The memory of the man from the diner followed the Question Marks for the next few days, like a shadow trailing them from class to class, from school to home and back again. None of them could stop thinking about what he'd said—that there was more to the Timekeepers than they knew. The unfinished conversation had left them curious, determined, and freaked-out all at the same time.

As a result, during free moments that week, Viola scoured the Internet for any more information about the Timekeepers of Moon Hollow. Unfortunately, she found nothing more than she had the first time she'd looked. Rosie was drawn to research too, but instead of going after the supposed secrets of the town's secret society, she decided to try to find out more about the man they'd met at the diner. Phineas Galby had mentioned he was traveling upstate to visit family, but Rosie found no evidence of any Galbys anywhere in New York. The man had either made up the name, or he had virtually no Internet presence. Staying off-line, Woodrow and Sylvester did field work instead, literally, by going out into their yard, revisiting the spot where someone had dug a hole a couple weeks prior. On hands and knees, they picked through the grass, trying to find a clue they might have originally missed. But other than a weird-looking snail shell, they too turned up nothing.

If Mr. Galby had intended to stir the Question Marks' curiosity, he'd succeeded entirely. But it was difficult to know exactly what the man had intended, because he'd left no evidence of himself behind. None of them had even seen what kind of car he drove. They figured that he'd parked around the corner from the diner, leaving in the opposite direction of the window in which they'd been sitting.

When the four met later that week to share their lack of findings, they asked one another whether they believed Galby had actually been passing through town as he'd claimed or if maybe he'd sat at that table near them on purpose to listen in for a reason to approach them. Option two was obviously much creepier, but if that was the case, they knew that chances were high they might see him again. What they didn't know was whether or not that would be a good thing.

They played the Strangers Game using details of the man's appearance. His clothes had been worn-out and dirty—his fingernails too. Sylvester thought this might indicate that he didn't have a lot of money, but Viola wasn't so sure—the clothing itself had looked expensive. He'd even worn a tie. She imagined it was possible that Mr. Galby may simply have been out of his element. Maybe he wore dress clothes all the time, but had been digging around in filthy places and messed up his outfit. If that were the case, Rosie suggested, then he could have been looking for something; and if that were true, Woodrow added, maybe he'd sought them out hoping to learn if the Question Marks had the information he needed to find it.

"I'll bet anything that Mr. Galby was the one who dug up our backyard," said Woodrow. "If only we could prove it."

Viola was relieved on Friday night when her father came home from his office with a very cool mystery to share with her. And the group was excited the next morning, when she invited them all over to help her solve it. A new mystery is always a great distraction—especially from another, more difficult mystery that has you stumped.

*1*8

THE CRIME OF THE FIGURINE THIEF
(A ????? MYSTERY)

"Someone broke into my dad's office this week," said Viola. She was perched on her bed. Her friends surrounded her, lounging on the floor.

"Whoa," said Sylvester. "Is he okay?"

"He wasn't there at the time, thank goodness. But of course, he was freaked out when he discovered he'd been robbed."

"Robbed?" Rosie asked. "What kinds of things does your dad have in his office that someone would want to take?"

"Antiques," said Viola. "I love hanging out in there because there's always something to look at. His shelves are full of weird old books with gross pictures of medical oddities. There are relics from archaeology digs that he keeps underneath bell jars. He's also got a whole bunch of plants sitting on the windowsill, where they soak up the sun. But unfortunately the one really valuable item was the object the thief had set his or her sights on."

"What was it?" Woodrow asked.

"An old stone figurine of a goddess from ancient Mesopotamia."

"No way!" said Sylvester. "That's so cool . . . and *terrible* that someone stole it."

"It stands about a foot tall and weighs about twenty-five pounds. My dad kept it on a shelf behind his big oak desk, next to a few other cool artifacts. He figured it was safe there, because of all the security."

"Like the officers in the gatehouse at the campus's entrance," said Sylvester. "The one across the street from the Clintock Clock."

"Right," said Viola. "There's also a guard who sits at a desk just inside the entrance of my dad's building. There are cameras in all the hallways. And you have to have a key to get into any of the offices, like the one my dad uses."

"If the security is so high," Rosie said, "then how did someone manage to break in?"

"That's the big question," said Viola. "My dad was astounded when he went to work yesterday morning. He used his key to unlock the door. Inside, he didn't immediately notice anything wrong. He said he grabbed his watering can from the windowsill because his plants were looking thirsty. He noticed that all their leaves had turned away from the glass. But before he had a chance to fill the can, he realized that the figurine was gone. After a quick search of the room, he realized that someone must have taken it."

"So, what'd he do?" Sylvester asked.

"His teacher's assistant, a girl named Mallory, is the one other person who has a key to the office, so the first thing he did was call her to see if she knew anything about it. Mallory was as shocked as my father. She said that she'd finished up her work the night before and had locked the door on her way out. My dad knew that was true because he'd unlocked the door on his way in. Next, my dad went to the college security office and reported the incident. The officer in charge, this guy named Stu, seemed pretty confident that they would be able to catch the thief immediately."

"Why was Officer Stu so confident?" asked Sylvester.

"Every hallway has a security camera in it," said Woodrow. "The officer probably thought that if someone had come in after Mallory had left for the night, it would be caught on video."

"Right," said Viola. "So the officer pulled the footage from the night before. The video showed Mallory leaving around eight o'clock, just like she'd said. My dad said she was only carrying a few file folders, and he was sure that she wasn't hiding the figurine under her coat—it was too big. Not that he believed she would have been capable of stealing."

"I'm guessing the video didn't show anyone else coming in or out of your dad's office," said Rosie.

Viola shook her head. "Nope. My dad cleans the office himself. Other than Mallory, no one else has access. And that's the real mystery. How the heck did someone get in and steal the figurine without being caught on tape?"

Sylvester, Rosie, and Woodrow squirmed on Viola's bedroom floor as they tried to work out an answer. After a few seconds, Woodrow spoke up. "Maybe the thief somehow messed with the camera? Could they have broken into your dad's office, then found the security footage and somehow destroyed the evidence of the crime?"

"That sounds really complicated," said Rosie. "I have an idea that seems much more plausible. A way that someone could steal the figurine, but

"Through the office window," said Rosie.

"That's what my dad came up with," replied Viola. "In fact, after Officer Stu ruled out the door entry, my dad remembered something he'd seen in the room earlier that clued him in that a window had been opened. *Can you think of my dad's clue?*"

Rosie nodded. "You mentioned that when your dad came into the room, the leaves on his plants were turned away from the glass. But you also said that the plants usually like to soak up the sunlight. Most plant leaves will turn *toward* their light source, so if they were facing away from the glass, that would indicate that someone had moved them. The thief needed access to the window, and the plants were in the way."

"You're right," said Viola. "And that was the story my father told me last night when he came home from work. The police are still unsure of who did it."

"So, your dad asked you to help him figure out who the thief was?" said Sylvester.

Viola smiled and nodded. "He knew we might be able to help him out."

"Ha!" said Woodrow. "Your dad's so cool. Did you give him an answer?"

"Not yet. I wanted to get everyone else's input. So what do you think? Do we have enough information here to figure out how to catch the thief and maybe find my dad's artifact?"

"I think so," said Rosie. "In fact, I'm pretty sure I know who the thief is."

Viola sat up. ***"Really? Who?"***

"Mallory," said Rosie, keeping her voice low.

"No way," said Sylvester. "The video showed that she was innocent."

"The video showed that Mallory didn't leave the office with the figurine," said Rosie. "But that doesn't mean she didn't take it."

"If I tell my dad that Mallory is the main suspect, he's going to want proof." Viola frowned. ***"So, what's the proof that Mallory is our villain?"***

"Can I give it a try?" said Woodrow. Rosie waved at him to continue. "Mallory was the only other person with a key to your dad's office. She was the last one to leave the office last night. The video proves that. We also know that she didn't leave with the figurine—the figurine had to have left via the window. But I don't think our thief actually came in through the window."

"What?" asked Sylvester. "How do you figure that?"

"Viola's dad or the police would have noticed if the window had been broken . . . or if it had been unlocked," Woodrow continued. "And although the plants had been moved, they were still on the windowsill when Mr. Hart arrived in the morning. So, they'd been moved—but they'd also been moved back. And the window had been unlocked—and then locked again."

"Which could only have been done from the inside," Rosie added.

"Right," said Woodrow. "Mallory must have unlocked the window, moved the plants out of the way, and then dropped the figurine out onto the lawn. Then before leaving, she replaced the plants on the windowsill, locked both the window and the door, and strolled out of the building . . . and around the corner, to where her prize was waiting."

"Wow," said Viola. "I wonder why she did it. Money? I bet if we tell our theory to my father, he'd confront her. Maybe he can even get the figurine back!"

"Either that," said Sylvester, "or he could just tell the police."

"I guess so," answered Viola. "But knowing my dad, he'll probably want to take care of the situation himself. Threat of a ruined reputation may inspire Mallory to do what's right. Right?"

19

THE SORROW OF HAL-MUH-NI
(A ??? MYSTERY)

By mid-December, the Timekeepers hullabaloo had nearly died out, and the Question Marks finally felt like their lives had gotten back to normal—as normal as their lives could be. The mystery of Phineas Galby still hung above them like an icicle waiting to fall, but they'd heard nothing more from him since the night at the diner.

Little things came up—like locating a classmate's missing pencil and guessing who passed gas during math class—but the group agreed that instances like these weren't worth a serious club meeting.

A couple of weeks before Christmas, Sylvester's grandmother took a bus trip across the state to visit her sister in Buffalo. After a couple days, Sylvester realized that he missed having her around. And missing her had nothing to do with the money she kept slipping him. Sylvester put it all in his sock drawer, but he couldn't bring himself to spend it. It didn't really feel like his money at all.

Several days after she'd left on her trip, Sylvester woke in his basement bedroom while it was still dark out. He felt especially itchy. After turning on the lamp next to his bed, he flipped the covers away to see strange bumps all over his stomach. They looked like bites, similar to the ones that he'd discovered on his ankles a few weeks earlier. Little red dots were lined up in rows, as if some insect had made its way along his skin, chomping every few steps. The sight disturbed him so much that he ran upstairs and woke his parents.

When his mother saw the marks, her eyes widened. They all paraded back downstairs. His parents pulled the bottom sheet from the mattress. Looking closely at the stitching along the edges, they recoiled, gasping and stepping quickly away from the bed. "Oh my gosh," said his mom.

"What's wrong?" asked Sylvester.

"Oh, honey," she answered, "you can't stay down here."

Sylvester knew it had something to do with what they'd found on his mattress, or *in* his mattress. His stomach went sour. Still, he managed to ask, "Why not?"

"Bedbugs!" Woodrow cried, immediately scooting away from Sylvester at the lunch table. It was the same reaction Sylvester had had the

134

night before, when his parents finally told him what had invaded his bedroom. "That's so creepy!"

"Yeah," said Sylvester, red-faced. *"I know that."*

"Where did they come from?" said Viola.

"Funny you should ask," said Sylvester. "Because my parents wondered the same thing. We've never had bedbugs in our house before. So they probably weren't just hanging out in my basement, waiting for me. ***Where do you think they came from?"***

"They must have hitched a ride on your grandmother's stuff," said Rosie, tugging at her braids with worry. "The Oriental rug doesn't seem to have enough crevices for the bugs to hide in . . . so it might have been the yellow couch that your grandmother seems to love so much. Once down there, they migrated to your bed . . . and to their food source. You!"

"Yup," said Sylvester. "That's what my mom figured out last night. She did a quick search of the couch and found the creepy little monsters all along the cushion seams. So nasty. I couldn't shower enough last night, or this morning. But my parents don't think the bugs have spread outside of the basement yet."

"I didn't know they really existed," said Woodrow. "I thought they were imaginary creatures from that old nursery rhyme: *Good night, sleep tight, don't let the bedbugs bite.*"

"Oh, they're real all right," said Sylvester. "And let me tell you straight up: That nursery rhyme does *not* work. If the bedbugs want to bite, there's nothing you or I can do to stop them."

"But what are you going to do about it?" asked Viola. "I heard that bedbugs are really hard to get rid of."

"My parents already called an exterminator. And we're going to wash all our clothes. But most important, my parents called the dump to take away my grandmother's yellow couch."

"But your grandmother was so attached to that couch," said Rosie. "What did she say when they told her they had to trash it?"

"I don't know. They were going to call her this morning. I wasn't around to hear the fallout." Sylvester shuddered. "I don't want her to be upset or anything, but there is no way I was spending one more night in that basement knowing little bugs were sucking my blood."

"Really?" said Woodrow. "Sounds like the kind of thing you'd enjoy."

Sylvester squinted, then punched Woodrow in the shoulder.

Woodrow glanced at the girls for support. Viola replied, "Sorry, but you pretty much deserved that."

When Sylvester got home from school that afternoon, he quickly checked the basement. The couch was gone. "Sylvester!" his mother called. "I'm in the laundry room."

He came back upstairs, peeked in at her, and said, "Need help?" His mother was frantically folding clothes in the small room off the kitchen where the washer and dryer hummed.

She shook her head. "Yes, but not with this stuff. When your father called Hal-muh-ni this morning to tell her what happened, she went ballistic."

"Ballistic? That sounds bad."

"She insisted that your father retrieve the couch immediately. He told her that was impossible. Honestly, I can't understand her attachment to this piece of furniture." Mrs. Cho shrugged. "But it's undeniable. I'd like you to be here this evening when she gets home so you can help us try to calm her down."

"She's coming home today? What about her visit?"

"She left her sister's house early. That's how important this is to her." Mrs. Cho sighed, frustrated, and launched herself into folding shirt after shirt after shirt.

"Where'd you get all this money?" Viola gasped. It was later in the afternoon. The group had decided to meet in Rosie's dining room. Sylvester wore a freshly washed, bug-free sweatshirt and pair of corduroys. With a dramatic flourish, he'd tossed several twenty-dollar bills onto the table.

"I haven't told anyone about this," said Sylvester, "because Hal-muh-ni asked me not to. But recently, a few times, I've found her in my bedroom. And whenever I do, she hands me a wad of cash. She's told me that it's a gift, that she wanted to leave it under my pillow. But with all the drama going on now, I have a different idea about what she's been doing with that money."

"She's not a con artist, is she?" said Woodrow. Sylvester rolled his eyes and shook his head. Woodrow continued, "Then what is Hal-muh-ni's deal? *What has she really been doing down in the basement with that money?*"

"Making withdrawals," said Sylvester.

"You mean, like, bank withdrawals?" Viola asked. Sylvester nodded. "She was keeping money in the old yellow couch?"

"That's what I assume," said Sylvester. "It must be her savings."

"Oh no!" said Rosie. "That's awful. What was she thinking, keeping all that cash in your house?"

"I'm not sure," said Sylvester. "She doesn't trust banks or something. I just figured it out this afternoon, and I finally told my mom all about it. Of course, now I'm going to have to give the money back. Whatever. I shouldn't have accepted it anyway. But losing this money is nothing compared to what Hal-muh-ni might lose if my dad doesn't track down that couch. I asked if I could go with him to the town dump to help look for it, but my parents didn't want me digging around in the dirt . . . so here I am."

"Is there anything we can do to help?" Viola asked.

"Keep your fingers crossed for her. For all of us, I guess." Woodrow, Rosie, and Viola did just that, all night. In fact, they woke up with sore knuckles.

The next morning at school, Sylvester pulled the other three aside before classes started, so he could explain what had happened the night before.

"So, just as the sun was setting, my dad ended up at the dump in the hills past Deerhof Park," Sylvester started. "He talked to the manager, an old man named Ned, about where the latest large furniture drop-offs might be located. Ned looked at my dad like he had two heads, but pointed him in the right direction. Near the rear lot. When my dad drove all the way back there, he realized that someone already had his eye on the couch. In fact, my dad said this person had already loaded the couch onto the bed of a small busted-up pickup truck. He immediately recognized this person. And he told me that I would recognize him too, given the chance."

"Was it Bill?" asked Woodrow, with a determined look. "I knew he was up to something!"

"No," said Sylvester, rolling his eyes. ***"So, if it wasn't your mom's boyfriend, who was trying to take my grandmother's couch away from the dump?"***

Rosie and Viola thought for a while. Then, Viola's eyes lit up. "Yesterday afternoon, Sylvester said his parents didn't want him digging around in the dirt at the dump," she said. "And who have we seen recently who looked like he's spent some time digging around?"

"Phineas Galby?" said Rosie, shocked.

Sylvester raised his eyebrows. "Yup."

"The guy from the diner?" said Woodrow. "That can't be a coincidence. He must have known what was inside the couch."

Sylvester shrugged. "Thankfully, my father had the guts to confront Phineas. They argued about the couch, then my dad managed to wiggle past him and hop up on the bed of the truck. He patted down the cushions and realized that one felt different than the others. When he unzipped it, he found a small canvas sack, filled with rolls of cash. My grandmother's savings. Mr. Galby was paralyzed with shock, so my dad managed to get back to his car and drive off, leaving Galby behind with the yellow couch . . . and the bedbugs."

Woodrow suddenly looked like someone had struck him on the back of the head.

"What's wrong?" Viola asked.

"The hole at the Four Corners," Woodrow answered slowly. "Phineas *was* the one who dug it. We figured he might be looking for something.

Was it Hal-muh-ni's money that he wanted all along?"

"Could be," said Viola. "But then, what was with the stuff he told us at the diner—about the Timekeepers and how we supposedly don't know much about them?"

"And how did he know about your grandmother's money in the first place?" asked Woodrow. "Unless he was watching through the basement windows. . . ."

Sylvester grimaced. "I don't want to think about that."

"Either way," said Viola, "I'm still willing to bet that whatever Phineas was seeking originally was not an old woman's savings account."

"So, then what was he *really* looking for?" Sylvester asked. "And now that my dad stole back Phineas's consolation prize, what if Phineas returns to try and find whatever he wanted in the first place?"

20

THE SLIPPERY SLOPES OF DEERHOF PARK

Snow arrived in Moon Hollow a few nights later for the first time that winter. The Question Marks awoke the morning after the storm to the joyful news that school had been canceled. The snow itself wasn't the problem—the town always plowed and salted the roads—but a light, dangerous layer of ice glossed the trees branches, the rooftops, the swing sets, and the sidewalks, turning the world to glass as the sun finally broke through the clouds sometime after breakfast.

The group brought sleds up the hill to Deerhof Park, which, according to Woodrow, was the best place within walking distance to catch swift speed and, if they were lucky, a few inches of flight.

In between races, Sylvester filled his friends in on the details of Hal-muh-ni's story. She was mortified to learn that the couch was infested. She had no idea where the bugs had come from. Rosie shrugged at that news. "Nature is the biggest mystery, isn't it?" she asked.

Sylvester's mom was currently trying to convince her to set up a bank account, to keep her

144

savings safe. In the meantime, Hal-muh-ni had decided to make two big investments. She paid for the Chos' exterminator. And she bought Sylvester a brand-new bed, so he wouldn't have to worry about bug bites anymore.

After a couple hours of sledding, the four were winded and feeling frozen, so they started home, hoping that grilled cheese sandwiches and tomato soup awaited them. They dragged their sleds behind them, laughing and slipping along the now worn grooves in the snow. Ahead, past the great white gazebo, a truck was parked along the side of the road. At first, they thought it looked like a stalled-out snowplow. But as the group came closer, they noticed its front fender wasn't rigged to clear streets. In fact, the truck was so beat-up, it looked like it shouldn't even be on the road. The engine's rattle was muffled by the white coating on the grass. Exhaust plumed from the tail pipe, gray smoke that disappeared within seconds in the cold air. Someone was sitting behind the wheel. He appeared to be watching them.

Even if they hadn't just been rolling around in the snow, they all would have felt the chill that now stopped them in their tracks.

"Maybe we should cut across the backyards between here and our street," Rosie suggested. The others agreed. Rather than proceeding toward the road, they made a sharp turn toward the trees. Instantly the driver's door on the truck popped open, and a large man stepped out. As he trudged toward them, his face became clear. It was Phineas Galby.

"Hold on," he called, raising a black mittened hand above his head.

The four were about to run, but Viola suddenly had a vision of them alone in the secluded woods. If they were going to confront this man, it would be best to do it where they had a chance of being seen by passersby. Viola turned back to him and called out, "What do you want?" hoping that her tone would force him to keep his distance. It worked. The man paused, standing in knee-deep snow between them and the road. He must have sensed that coming any closer might send them scattering away.

"I want to talk," he said. "Just to talk."

"Fine," said Viola. "Then maybe you'll tell us why you've been following us." It sounded like something someone would say in a mystery novel. She felt momentarily proud of herself. "It wasn't for Sylvester's grandmother's money, was it?"

The man chuckled. "No. It wasn't. Well . . . not at first. And not anymore."

"Then what do you want to talk about?" said Sylvester, his voice shaking.

"Come on," said the man, with a hint of frustration, "don't tell me you kids don't know." The four glanced at one another. Know what? "Look, you can play dumb, but the innocence game is not going to work forever. You must have it, and if you don't have it, then at the very least, you must know where it is."

"What is *it*?" said Woodrow.

The man threw his hands in the air. One of his large mittens flew off and landed in the snow. He didn't seem to notice or care. "The Timekeepers' treasure . . . Tell me where I can find it."

Timekeepers' treasure? None of them knew what to say or do.

Finally Rosie spoke up. "We'll never tell you anything."

Woodrow, Sylvester, and Viola whipped their heads to look at her. "But we don't *know* anything," Sylvester whispered through his teeth.

"Shh," she answered. Rosie folded her arms awkwardly across her puffy pink coat. Though it took an extreme amount of will, she didn't budge, not even when the man stepped toward them.

Phineas reached into his pocket and pulled out a piece of paper. Wearing a look of consternation, he quickly unfolded the ratty, crumbling white leaf. He held it up and shook it at them. "My grandfather was a member of the Timekeepers. This page is proof—his membership agreement. I found it with his things after he passed away." The paper fluttered in the icy breeze. "When I was your age, he told me secret stories—tales he made me promise never to share with anyone. He explained that he and his friends had hidden away a priceless treasure. He said that when the last of the Timekeepers was gone, the treasure would belong to the town. But when the final member of the club died, something must have gone wrong. As far as I can tell, the town never learned of what it was meant to inherit. I've traveled here to Moon Hollow at least once a year since then, looking for clues about what my grandfather's friends left behind. I was beginning to lose hope . . . until you four discovered the clues in the clocks. I've been following you ever since. I thought the cash in that old couch might have been the secret, that you kids had discovered the treasure and kept it for yourselves. But now I realize I was wrong." He clenched his bare fist. "You must know where the real treasure is, and you still refuse to show it to the rightful heir."

Even after this flood of information, Viola managed to speak up. "But you're not the heir. You said it yourself: The Timekeepers meant for their treasure to go to the town. Not in your pocket."

The man looked like he'd been caught stealing candy. "What's the town going to do with it? Buy some more *clocks*?"

"Excuse me, sir," said Woodrow, "but I don't believe that's really your decision."

The man closed his eyes and took a deep breath. "Tell you what. You show me where the treasure is, and I'll split it with you. You can keep ten percent. Deal?"

"Deal."

Woodrow, Sylvester, and Viola once again stared at Rosie in shock. She whispered so only they could hear. "He won't leave us alone unless we agree." She turned back to the man and called to him, "But not today."

"Why not?" said the man.

"The treasure is . . . too difficult to get to," Rosie said, her resolve beginning to crack. She hadn't planned this part out.

Viola took over. "We'll meet you at the library on Monday afternoon. Three o'clock. You'll get everything that's coming to you. We promise."

By the time they reached Viola's front yard, each of them was out of breath. They all collapsed into the snow near the porch steps. They were enthralled and frightened, surprised and shocked, enchanted and nauseated. They had escaped their villain. But now they had to answer to him. They had no idea what to do.

"Why did you tell him to come back?" Sylvester asked Viola, sitting on the steps.

"It didn't matter what I told him." Viola sat beside him. "Do you really think he's just going to let us go about our business and not watch to see what we're up to? He's been keeping an eye on us for weeks, and we didn't even notice until recently. He'll show up at three o'clock on Monday, but that doesn't mean he won't show up before that."

"So, what are we going to do?" asked Woodrow, perched nearby on his sled in the snow-covered lawn. He rubbed at his red ears. "We don't know anything about this dude."

"He seemed sort of nuts," Sylvester said.

"You think?" said Rosie, brushing flakes from her coat. She froze, suddenly struck by an idea. "You guys?" The others looked at her, waiting for her to continue. "There is a *treasure* here in Moon Hollow!" Rosie said. "How cool is that?"

"And you think we should actually try and find it?" Sylvester replied, unsure.

"Phineas, or whatever his name is, has been looking for it for years with no luck," said Woodrow.

Viola shrugged, a smirk spreading across her lips. "Yeah, but he's not a member of the Question Marks Mystery Club, is he?"

21

THE HUNT FOR THE TIMEKEEPERS' TREASURE (A ?????? MYSTERY)

"So, where do we start?" said Rosie.

"We've already been all over town," said Sylvester.

"Where haven't we looked yet?" Woodrow asked.

Viola thought about that. "Maybe that doesn't matter." When her friends looked at her funny, she continued, "We didn't know there was a treasure until today. It's possible we've missed a clue or two in a few of the places we've already explored."

After a few seconds, all four said, "The library!"

Loading snacks from the Harts' kitchen into Viola's bag, the group tied their scarves tight and made their way into town. Despite the school closing, the library remained open, though it was nearly deserted. Rosie ran through the Clintock Gallery to tell her mom that the four of them were there. The others headed to the computer desks to come up with a plan. But when Rosie met them a few minutes later, she wore a look of surprise.

"What's wrong?" asked Sylvester.

"You mean, *What's right?*" said Rosie, smiling. "Follow me, you guys." She led the other three back to the main lobby, to the wall behind the security desk. The golden relief-sculptures glimmered in the icy sunlight that streamed through the large windows at the library's entrance. Rosie nodded at the brass marker bolted to the wall. Tarnished text indicated the title of the work: *Thirteen Capsules of Endurance.* It was dated 1936.

"On my way to say hi to my mom just now, the portraits in the Clintock Gallery caught my eye. Specifically, one name leaped out at me. I knew I'd read it somewhere else. Passing back through the lobby, I paused here, remembering why the name was familiar." Rosie pointed at the marker again, this time to the name of the artist, a woman named Pauline Emmett.

"The artist of these sculptures was a member of the Timekeepers?" asked Woodrow.

"So it would appear," said Rosie.

"Bingo!" said Sylvester.

Viola leaned close to the marker. Below Pauline's name was a note about the work from the artist herself. "Guys, take a look at this." The rest of them read silently along with Viola.

Thireen Capsules of Endurance is te culmination of nearly eight yars of mapping, planning, and hoping for pledges rom friends. These imges repesent the struggles and triuphs that our citizns have experienced since the incorporation of Moon Hollow in the year of nineteen hundred two. I created this work to help us remember what is missing and what we need to find. May the capsules lead us foward to our future.

Sylvester scoffed. "Pauline really needed to use spell-check before sending her letters off to be printed."

"Um . . . They didn't have computers back then," said Woodrow.

"That's no excuse," said Sylvester. "Or at least it wouldn't be in Mr. Glenn's English class."

"True," said Rosie. "The misspellings are so odd. How did they get engraved here?"

"They *are* odd." Viola chuckled. "Just plain odd . . . and what does that usually mean?"

"You think this marker is a clue?" Sylvester said.

"Don't you?" said Viola.

"It must be," said Rosie. "Like the portraits in the gallery were a clue."

"She made these sculptures to help us *remember what is missing*," said Woodrow in a low voice. "Look, she says so right there. If this is

"Letters," said Rosie. "Obviously."

"Exactly," said Woodrow. "Which ones?" The group looked at the message on the marker again.

"Hold on," said Viola, pulling her trusty notebook and pen from her bag. She wrote down the first sentence, circling the misspelled words.

"Thirteen. The. Years. From," Viola said.

"Do you think it's some kind of word scramble?" asked Rosie. "The years from thirteen? From the thirteen years?" she tried.

Viola shook her head. Then, she recited the missing letters. "*T* was missing from *thirteen*. *H* was missing from *the*. *E* from *years*. *F* from . . . well, *from*."

"Oh," said Rosie. "I see. *T. H. E. F.*"

"Thef?" said Sylvester. "What's that supposed to mean?"

"Nothing yet," said Woodrow. "Keep going, Viola."

"The *A* from *images*," she said. "Represent. Triu*m*phs. Citizens . . ."

"And the *R* in *forward*," finished Sylvester.

"That gives us *A. R. M. E. R*," Viola said. She glanced at her friends.

"I don't get it," said Sylvester. "Thef? Armer?"

"Put it together, silly," said Rosie.

"Oh!" said Sylvester. "The farmer!" He crinkled his brow. "Wait . . . Who is the farmer?"

Viola simply pointed up. It took the group a few seconds, but eventually they all caught on. The farmer was one of the "thirteen capsules," the golden relief-sculpture on the wall just over their heads. He wore stiff overalls and a look of hopeful determination as he seemed to stare out from the wall toward the windows at the front of the library. He held his small scythe out away from his body as if pointing at another image — a calf. The calf stretched his head back from the scythe, gazing at the wide-winged eagle near the ceiling.

"Okay," said Sylvester. "What are we supposed to do now?" He turned toward the direction of the farmer's gaze, facing the plaza and clock outside the library's front door. "Maybe this farmer dude is trying to tell us where we need to go next. Outside?"

"I think you're onto something," said Woodrow. "Except he doesn't want us to go outside . . . or at least the artist, Pauline, didn't. Check out the marker on the wall again. She says: *May the capsules lead us forward to our future.* ***If those are instructions, what is she telling us to do?"***

"Maybe the symbols on the wall are a map," said Rosie.

"Really?" said Sylvester, stepping back to get a better view of the whole picture.

Rosie went on. "Pauline must want us to start at the farmer. But what comes after that?"

"The farmer's scythe is pointing at the calf," said Viola. "And what's the calf looking at?"

"The eagle!" said Sylvester. "And the eagle's gazing at the salmon in the kneeling woman's hands."

"And the salmon came from the stream . . . and on and on," said Woodrow, moving along the wall from left to right, as the images brought him closer to the opposite side of the room. "Symbol by symbol. And we come to 'capsule' number twelve." He pointed up at a great golden sun that hovered near the left side of the wall. "What's the sun shining on?"

"The sundial," said Rosie. "The thirteenth capsule. That's where the trail stops."

"Ha," Sylvester chuckled, "another clock."

"There must be a clue here," said Viola, standing underneath the sundial symbol. "Look closely. Do you guys see anything that might help us?"

"Yes!" said Woodrow. "Check it out." Poking from the top of the sundial's little spire was a familiar sight: a shiny acorn."

"Wow," said Rosie. They all considered this new development in silence for a moment. *"Knowing what we know about the acorn symbols we've found around town, what do you guys think this sundial is trying to tell us?"*

"This 'clock' has got to be an address," said Sylvester. "The acorn represents Oakwood Avenue. Pauline Emmett is pointing us to another location."

"But Oakwood is a long street," said Viola. "It runs down by the train tracks and then up into the hills. Where are we supposed to look?"

"Remember, the numbers the clocks got stuck on turned out to be street numbers," said Rosie.

"So," said Woodrow, "what time is this sundial stuck at?"

"It looks like it's pointing at four o'clock," said Viola. "Number four . . . Oakwood Avenue?"

After a quick map search on the Internet, the kids learned that 4 Oakwood Avenue was the Moon Hollow Museum, where Rosie's father worked. Rosie shook her head. "Well, at least we know we'll be able to get inside, even if the place is closed for the weather."

"But how are we going to know what to look for once we get there?" said Sylvester, bundling himself up before stepping outside into the cold.

"Same way we always do," said Viola. "By paying attention to the things other people ignore."

"I think we should also pay attention to anyone who might be following us," said Woodrow. "Especially anyone driving a beat-up pickup truck."

The hike to the museum would usually have taken about twenty minutes, but the group was slowed down by the now melting snow and ice. No one appeared to be following them, but they couldn't be sure. The day had clouded over and light seemed to be fading.

The four found the front door of the museum locked. "Shoot," said Sylvester. "What do we do now?"

Rosie pursed her lips. "I might get in trouble for this . . . ," she said, then waved at the group to follow her around the side of the building. After passing a few windows, she stopped. In the window directly above them, a light glowed, casting a soft white box on the snow at their feet. "My dad's office." Rosie bent down and picked up some powder. She packed it loosely between her gloved fingers. Then, sighing nervously, she tossed the snowball at the glass. Seconds later, Mr. Smithers's face appeared, peering out at them. Rosie waved. Her father looked confused, but quickly motioned for them to go back around to the front of the building.

A few minutes later, they stood in the darkened museum lobby. "What are you kids doing here?" asked Rosie's father. "I know you're off from school, but we've closed early this afternoon."

Rosie glanced over her shoulder, thinking of that pickup truck she and her friends all hoped had left town. She wished she could tell her father everything that had happened that morning, but she didn't want to betray her friends and the decision they'd made together. They *had* to find the treasure, if only to protect it from Phineas Galby, and they couldn't risk their parents pulling them off the case.

Maybe instead of telling him everything, she decided, she could tell him part of it. "We need your help."

"Here it is," said Mr. Smithers. "Pauline Emmett." He'd led them to a small painting in a secluded corner of the museum, a room dedicated to the works of local artists. Nestled in a wide, ornately carved wooden frame, Ms. Emmett's artwork hung on the big white wall. Opposite, a large window overlooked the Hudson River. Outside, huge chunks of ice had broken up on the water and were floating downstream in alternating mosaic tiles of dark and light. The view itself was a work of art. "What was so important about this painting that you had to walk all the way out here today?" Mr. Smithers asked.

"I told you," said Rosie. "We're working on a case. Top secret." She glanced at the others. "We'll let you know later. Promise."

Mr. Smithers squinted and shook his head. He considered the painting for a second before turning away. "If you insist, darling daughter. Just don't touch anything!"

They all approached the Emmett watercolor, a dreamy, almost foggy view of the same river that

161

was directly behind them. "I'm confused," said Sylvester. "Is she saying that the treasure is in the river?"

"I doubt it," said Viola. "All the clues have been very specific until now. Maybe there's some sort of code in the image."

The group spent a few minutes thinking about the shapes of the mountains in the distance, the curve of the river itself. Maybe there were letters hidden in the composition, another secret message of sorts. But they noticed nothing except the purposefully atmospheric nature of the image.

"Do you guys think that maybe this painting is the treasure?" said Rosie. "Could it be that simple?"

"That's possible," said Sylvester. "But why would the Timekeepers go to all this trouble just to display their secret 'treasure' on the wall of a museum? It doesn't add up."

"You're right," said Woodrow. "It doesn't. But I think right now, we're looking a little bit too closely to see the answer."

"What do you mean?" said Viola. Woodrow took a step backward, away from the wall, and motioned his friends to follow. "We're staring right at the clue, and the painting is not it."

Sylvester bristled. "There's nothing else on this wall. What else should we be looking at?"

"There's more here than just a painting." Woodrow smiled. *"Viola? Rosie? Do you guys see what I see?"*

"The frame!" Viola cried. "Look. There. In the top left and bottom right corners. Carvings of maple leaves."

"That's it," said Rosie. Several tree branches were carved into the frame. Three small leaves decorated the branch at the top. Four were at the bottom. "Our next clue. Maple Avenue!"

"But again," said Sylvester with a smirk, "I ask . . . where?"

"Darn it," Viola said. "There's definitely no clock in this painting. So how are we supposed to figure out the address this time?"

"The clue wasn't in the painting," said Woodrow. "It was in the frame."

"So the address must be in the frame too," said Rosie. She stared intently at the wood.

"Yup," said Woodrow. "It's right in front of us. **Don't you see it?**"

"Oh," said Sylvester, "you're right. Three maple leaves at the top. Four at the bottom. The address must be number thirty-four. So clever."

"We were just there!" said Viola.

"Sort of," Rosie replied. "The library's at number fifty-five, remember. Thirty-four must be a little farther down the street."

"Near the bank where Bill works," said Woodrow. He squinted as an idea came to him. "Huh . . . I think I have an idea of where we need to go next."

"Where?" said the rest of the group.

Woodrow smiled. "You'll see," he teased.

By the time the Question Marks made it back to Mr. Smithers's office, he was packing up to leave for the day. "I can drive you back into town," he said. "But you have to promise me you won't be getting into trouble."

"Dad!" Rosie cried, trying to answer him as vaguely as possible. She didn't want to lie to her father. Besides, she *also* hoped they wouldn't be getting into trouble.

A block before they reached the Moon Hollow Library, Rosie asked her father to let them out. He pulled up to the curb. "Don't be too much longer," he said. "I don't want you kids out walking on these roads in this weather." He waved good-bye, then drove off with a short honk.

They stood before One Cent Savings and

Trust. Lights were on in the bank. "Is Bill working today?" asked Sylvester.

Woodrow rolled his eyes. "Don't know. Don't care."

"But aren't we going inside?" said Rosie. "Maybe he can help us."

"The frame told us to go to number thirty-four Maple Avenue." Woodrow nodded at the number above the bank's front door. Thirty-six. "Wrong address."

Viola stepped away from the building to get a better view of the street. "Then we need to go next door to—"

"The abandoned storefront," said Woodrow. "I think this used to be . . . huh." He chuckled, reading the faded gold paint that was chipping from the store's window. "Clintock's watch repair store."

"How did we not notice this before?" said Viola, trying to contain her excitement.

"Even if we had," said Sylvester, "it wouldn't have meant what it does now." He went up to the front door. Inside, the store was pitch-dark. Dust coated the glass. Litter and snow had blown through a rusted accordion gate into the main vestibule. Behind the gate, the door was shut, a faded curtain drawn closed.

Rosie began, "How are we supposed to—" when Sylvester reached for the gate and tried to tug it open. To everyone's surprise, it gave way and slid open. "That's weird." Next, Sylvester tried the doorknob. It turned in his hand.

"Wait," said Viola. "We promised Mr. Smithers we'd be careful. Is it the smartest thing to go in by ourselves?"

Before anyone had the chance to answer, a gust of wind came up the street, snatching the knob out of Sylvester's grip. The door squeaked open, a stale scent wafted out, and the full darkness of the old store revealed itself to them. The group gave a collective sigh, knowing what they had to do. Pausing before the accordion gate, Viola glanced over her shoulder, making sure no one was watching them. She paid special attention to any cars that might be nearby—looking closely for Mr. Galby's ugly truck. But the street was clear. And with the sun beginning to disappear, the town had turned an eerie shade of blue, as if someone had spread watercolor paint all over Moon Hollow's snow white canvas. Holding her breath, she followed her friends inside.

A few moments later, their eyes began to adjust to the lack of light. The store was crowded with empty glass cases that were, they imagined, once filled with timepieces for sale.

"What was that?" said Sylvester, backing up against the nearest case. "I heard a noise." He nodded to the far wall, where another doorway opened upon a dark hallway. "It sounded like footsteps."

"Is someone here?" Rosie whispered, edging close to Viola.

"That would explain why the front door was open," said Viola.

"What do we do?" Sylvester asked. No one wanted to move. They all listened for a few more seconds.

"Maybe it's an animal," said Rosie. "A mouse or a squirrel."

"Or a rabid raccoon?" said Sylvester. "I don't know about this."

"We probably scared it off, whatever it was," Woodrow said.

"Or whoever?" Viola said, blowing into her hands to warm them. "We've come this far. We can't stop now." She stepped forward. "Hello?" she called to the darkness.

"What are you doing?" Sylvester whispered harshly.

"Trying to figure out what's going on here," Viola answered. "I checked outside for Mr. Galby's truck. If someone is here, it's not him."

"That's pretty shoddy reasoning," said Sylvester. "I don't want to end up locked in here. Or worse!"

Viola was fed up with chasing clues. She wanted answers—now. She stepped toward the dark hallway. "I wish I'd brought my flashlight."

"Me too," said Sylvester, following close behind.

They crept slowly forward, feeling their way along the tight corridor. Shortly, they found themselves in a large, empty room. It didn't seem like anyone was hiding in here, which made them instantly feel better. In the darkness, they made out a couple curtained windows in the far wall. Viola went over and pulled the curtains open; the shades fluttered noisily at the tops of the window frames. Dim light now filtered through the dirty glass, and the group could see the room in which they stood. A long metal desk against one wall indicated that once upon a time, this place must have been a work area. A small toolbox sat on one end of the table.

Maybe it was that there was not much else in the room to explore, but Viola was drawn toward the box on the table. The other three followed. She used her fingers to brush the thick layer of dust from the top of the container. It looked like it hadn't been opened in some time.

"What's inside?" Sylvester asked. Silently they all wondered the same thing: Were they about to uncover the treasure?

"One way to find out," said Woodrow.

"You do the honors, Viola," said Rosie. "You're the one who had the guts to come in here."

Viola lifted the lid. The hinges squeaked as the cover swung open. She sighed when she saw the contents. Tools in a toolbox? Big surprise. She felt she should have known better. Behind her, the group tensed. They were just as disappointed.

"Hold on," said Sylvester, tapping Viola on the shoulder. "Can I see?" He stepped closer to the table, peering into the container. "This looks familiar. My magic kit is set up the same way. Look, the floor of the box isn't as deep as it should be, which means . . ." He reached into the box and felt along the sides. "There's a false bottom." He pulled up on a small drawer that had been nestled inside. "There is more hidden here. Underneath." He grabbed something from the box's secret compartment and held it up for his friends to see. It was an old-fashioned-looking key.

"Holy cow," said Woodrow. Viola and Rosie silently shook their heads in disbelief.

"Where does it fit?" Sylvester asked, glancing around the room. The light outside was growing ever dimmer. Streetlights flickered on across the back alley, casting long swatches of illumination and ominous shadow through the windows. "There's nothing here to open."

"Maybe what it opens isn't in this room," said Woodrow.

"Can I see it?" Rosie asked. Sylvester handed her the key. After a few seconds, she looked up at her friends, her mouth parted in shock. She said nothing. Instead, she simply held the key up into the light from outside. They all observed what Rosie had: At the top of the key, three images had been sculpted into an elaborate, intertwined pattern.

Viola spoke, enchanted. "The cherry. The leaf. The acorn."

"A final clue?" said Woodrow. "Telling us where to find the lock that will reveal the treasure of the Timekeepers?"

"Maybe," said Rosie. "Hopefully."

Sylvester threw his hands into the air. ***"So, where the heck is this lock?"***

Woodrow didn't even wait to answer. "Up the street."

Rosie nodded. "At the library."

"*And* at the train station," Viola added.

Sylvester gasped. "*And* near the college's entry gate?"

The rest of them nodded. "The clocks," said Rosie.

"The cherry. The leaf. The acorn," said Viola. "All the streets. All the addresses. All of the Timekeepers' clues led us to this discovery. It was like they wanted someone to find what they'd hidden."

"So, what are we waiting for?" said Sylvester. "Let's go get it!"

Outside, the glow of the streetlights turned the snow into a dreamlike orange sorbet. This color against the darkening sky made the town look candy coated, almost too sweet. Too safe. The roads were empty; the entire world was quiet. The group dashed up the block, toward the clock in the center of the library's plaza. They were too enthralled to notice the familiar pickup truck parked across the street from the diner.

They crossed Main Street and finally reached their destination. The library was now closed, the windows dark. The tall clock appeared to be staring up and down the street, on the lookout for danger. The half-moon window, through which the cherry peeked, grinned as if congratulating them on their hard work. "Right back where we started," said Viola quietly, almost to herself.

Rosie clutched the key in her hand. For a moment, the object seemed to throb, but then Rosie realized it was her heart making her feel this way. "Look," she whispered. "Near the base. A small hole. A perfect fit."

"Do it," said Sylvester.

Someone coughed, and the group froze. They immediately knew that they were not alone. Stepping from the shadows, Phineas Galby appeared, wearing a wide, frightening smile. He held his hands out to them. "You have something for me?"

Rosie spoke up, saying the first thing that came to mind. "But it's not Monday yet."

"I don't care what day it is," said Phineas. "I want what belongs to me." He began to walk forcefully toward them. He was no longer playing games. The clock was the only thing between him and the Question Marks.

Woodrow shouted, "Run!"

Slipping on the snow, the group turned and ran back in the direction of the abandoned store. Phineas huffed and puffed not far behind them. They reached Main Street, unsure which way to go. They needed a place to hide. But Phineas's footsteps were coming closer. Leading the way,

Woodrow was about to head toward the diner when a voice called out from across the street.

"Woodrow!" It was Bill. He stood just outside One Cent Savings and Trust. Woodrow had never been so happy to see him. The group raced toward the bank, leaving Phineas flabbergasted and out of breath on the other side of the road. Bill stared for a few intense seconds at the man who'd been chasing the kids. Then as if flipping a switch, he greeted the group jovially. "Your mom's been looking for you!" he said loudly, as if he wanted Phineas to hear him. "Enough games for today. You kids must be freezing. Come inside." He nodded at the bank. Then, glancing back across the street, he called to Phineas, "And good night to you. Hope you make it safely back to where you belong. Roads in these parts can be dangerous on nights like these."

Woodrow's throat began to close. Why was Bill talking to Phineas as if he knew him? Suddenly, he wasn't sure following Bill was the best idea either. But now, what choice did they have?

The bank was warm. Bill told them to wait in his office while he closed up.

After a few seconds, Sylvester spoke up. "What the heck just happened?"

Still clutching the key, Rosie shook her head. "I knew we should have told our parents what was happening. About the treasure."

173

"Treasure?" said a female voice from the hall-way outside the office. The door swung the rest of the way open. When they saw who was there with Bill, the Question Marks all stood. Shocked. Ms. Dzielski, their principal, wore a long black coat. She crossed her arms and bit her bottom lip. "What treasure?"

Bill sighed. "Margaret, we don't need to con-fuse them any more than we already have. They've come this far. Now it's time we gave them answers."

As it turned out, the man who called himself Phineas Galby was not the only one who'd been tracking the Question Marks on their journey through Moon Hollow that day. Another group had been paying close attention to them ever since their discovery of Clintock's clock clues at the beginning of November.

Ms. Dzielski sat behind Bill's desk, looking just as authoritative as she had on the day she'd invited them into her office. Bill stood beside her. "Let me start by saying you've all behaved really irresponsibly," said the principal. "Sneaking around, not telling anyone what you were up to, especially after being approached by a complete stranger who obviously has some screws loose . . ."

Each of the four blushed, their faces burn-ing. Was she going to give them detention, make them write one-thousand-word essays, expel them? *Could* she even do that here, they wondered?

"Margaret," said Bill, with a hint of frustration, "we agreed."

Ms. Dzielski sighed. "Sorry. There's something you kids need to know. The society you 'discovered,' the Timekeepers of Moon Hollow . . . Well, they still exist."

"You're looking at two of them," said Bill.

"What?" said Woodrow, glancing up at his mom's new boyfriend, all of his suspicions suddenly confirmed.

"We've been keeping tabs on you four," Ms. Dzielski continued. "We needed to find out exactly what you knew about us. That's one of the reasons I asked you to my office a month ago."

"And is that why Bill kept asking me about the mysteries my friends and I try to figure out?" said Woodrow, trying to control his temper. "Is that why you started going out with my mom?"

Now it was Bill's turn to blush. "Of course not. You know your mother and I met each other before you guys took on the mystery of the clocks."

"But you still used my mom to get close to me," Woodrow insisted. "You said it yourself. You wanted to know what we knew—if we were keeping anything else a secret."

"You wanted to know if we knew anything about the treasure!" said Sylvester, sticking up for his friend.

Bill shook his head. "I'm sorry if that's what you think, Woodrow. But your mom and I would have become close even if the Timekeepers never existed."

Ms. Dzielski added, "It was our duty though, as members, to try to learn what we could. The secrets of the Timekeepers have never been compromised before. We are more than pleased with how you worked it all out. If it wasn't for your curiosity, we might never have learned the whereabouts of the first Timekeepers' so-called treasure."

The four were so shocked they couldn't move. "You mean, all this time, you didn't know where it was?" Woodrow managed to ask.

The principal shook her head. "Once Bill and I realized that you hadn't already discovered the treasure, we hoped that you'd eventually look for it. We could tell you were onto something today, and we've been watching with interest. When we saw you approaching from down the block, Bill snuck back inside the bank. I thought I'd have a better view from the old space next door, which is owned collectively by the Timekeepers. I didn't mean to leave the entrance unlocked—but then, I didn't expect that was where you were headed." She shrugged. "Once you were inside, I stayed quiet, hidden in the workroom closet. I was flabbergasted when you discovered that key and reasoned out what it opened. To think it had been right under our noses all along! After you left the store, I ran and told Bill what had happened. We were about to follow you there and reveal everything. But then that man showed up. He chased you. And plans changed. I'm sorry you had to go through that."

"What you four accomplished is astounding," said Bill. "Years ago, Mr. Clintock left a trail of clues leading to three parcels, which we now know the Timekeepers had hidden in each of his clocks. He hoped that the society would continue on forever, but in case it did not, I suppose he wanted to be sure that the parcels would not be lost. The clues were a long lost map, one we were unaware of—but you four followed it perfectly."

"Why did you trust us?" asked Viola.

"We spent plenty of time trying to learn if we could," said Bill. "You might remember that interview you all gave to that reporter, Darlene Reese, a few weeks ago? Haven't you wondered why the article was never published?"

"Yeah!" said Sylvester. "Whatever happened to her?"

"She's doing just fine," said Ms. Dzielski. "I know, because she's my sister, as well as a member of the Timekeepers. She lives in the hills on the outskirts of town."

"She's not a reporter?" Viola asked, disappointed.

Ms. Dzielski shook her head. "I'm sorry. We needed to find out if you knew any more than what you'd told the *Herald*."

"But what we learned is that you all want to help people," said Bill. "So do we. We tend to be a little more secretive than you four, but both of our groups are most definitely mysterious."

"Which brings us to the point of this conversation," said Ms. Dzielski. She glanced at Bill, who nodded at her. "We'd like to ask you to join us."

The group gasped.

"You want *us* to be Timekeepers?" said Woodrow.

"Why not?" asked Bill. "You've proven yourselves worthy. Besides, you already know so much about us."

"With your parents' permission, we'd love all of you to participate," said Ms. Dzielski.

"What would we have to do?" Viola asked.

"You could come to meetings," said Bill. "You know where they are, don't you?"

The four of them laughed.

"Or you could simply keep doing what you're doing," said Ms. Dzielski. "Being good detectives. Helping your friends, your families, the people of Moon Hollow—*that* is the spirit of the Timekeepers."

Viola, Sylvester, Rosie, and Woodrow all looked at one another. They didn't even need to speak, except to say one word all together: "Yes!"

"Good," said Ms. Dzielski. "I must make one request." She smiled at Rosie and held out her hand. "The key, please." Rosie gave it one last squeeze, then gave it back.

"I have a question," said Viola. "You implied Mr. Clintock's parcels are not exactly a real treasure. If they aren't a treasure, then what are they?"

Bill and the principal smiled. "What is it that the Timekeepers keep?" asked Bill.

Viola raised an eyebrow. "Time?"

"Exactly," said Ms. Dzielski. "And how does one keep time?"

"Clocks?" Woodrow answered.

The principal chuckled. "True, clocks literally keep time. But years ago, when Mr. Clintock put together his plans to help build up this town and make it as special a place as he could, he and his friends decided to mark the occasion. Inside each clock is a time capsule, filled with objects that every member thought was important to the time in which they lived."

"Phineas Galby said the Timekeepers' treasure was priceless," said Sylvester.

"*Priceless* is a relative term," answered Bill. "So is treasure. If we were to open the parcels, we'd probably find letters, newspaper clippings, maybe some trophies or toys. Little things that were important to the very first members of the group. Pieces of our shared history. Yes, the items inside might get some cash at auction. But not much."

"None of the parcels have been opened since Mr. Clintock and the original Timekeepers locked them away," said Ms. Dzielski. "We'd like to keep it that way."

22

THE TIME CAPSULES

So much can happen in only a few days.

On Friday evening after the snowstorm, the Question Marks Mystery Club waited at Woodrow's driveway for Bill to pick everyone up for the meeting at the college's gatehouse. He'd have to switch cars with Mrs. Knox for the evening in order for all five of them to fit, but she didn't have a problem with that.

In fact, when Bill had asked each of their parents if Woodrow, Sylvester, Viola, and Rosie could join the Timekeepers of Moon Hollow, he was met with mild disbelief. All were surprised to hear not only that the "secret society" still existed, but that Bill was a senior member. But once he explained what the group was all about, the parents allowed their children to decide.

Obviously, they'd already made their decision.

Most of the snow had melted, but Bill drove slowly up into the hills, watchful for black ice. He parked on Cherry Tree Lane, not far from the gatehouse. When everyone got out, they noticed a small group of people huddled across the street from the college entrance on the small patio where one of Clintock's clocks stood. The four recognized some faces from around town, including Principal Dzielski's sister, Darlene, who eventually apologized to the Question Marks for her deception. Viola thought it was cool that this group had been able to keep themselves a secret for such a long time. What must they have thought when the Question Marks had uncovered the clues in the clock? For the first time since learning that the Timekeepers were still around, Viola felt embarrassed. She and her friends had caused such trouble for them!

Yesterday, the man who had called himself Phineas Galby was caught by police after trying to smash the clock face at the library. He insisted to them that there was a great treasure hidden inside. His argument didn't help him, and he was currently being held in the Moon Hollow Police station. Luckily, the clock survived without a crack.

Tonight, a small ladder was propped up against the side of the Cherry Tree Lane clock. Ms. Dzielski stood nearby. The group of Timekeepers parted as they noticed Bill coming up the street with the Question Marks. "Everyone ready?" Bill asked.

The principal held up the key that Sylvester had found in the toolbox in the abandoned store on Maple Avenue. Then she knelt down at the base of the clock. She inserted the key into the small hole there, and turned it to the right. A soft mechanical sound filled the icy night air. A motor whirred inside the bulbous clock head, then with an almost inaudible click, one of the faces unlocked, revealing a small dark gap. An older gentleman—Viola recognized him as Mr. Fredericks, owner of a local antiques shop— stepped up on the ladder and pulled the clock face the rest of the way open. Inside, gears and cogs glinted, reflecting ghostly light from nearby streetlamps. Mr. Fredericks reached inside, into a gap underneath the clockworks, and pulled out a large wooden box. He handed the box to someone else on the ground.

"One down," said Ms. Dzielski. "Two to go."

The Timekeepers traveled to the other clocks around town, using the key to remove the other parcels. After what Phineas Galby had done, everyone understood how vulnerable the "treasures" were. It was time to make a change. Mr. Clintock's clues had certainly worked as a map. The Question Marks had tested it out. But in order to protect the time capsules now, they needed to be moved. Bill set up three large safety deposit boxes at One Cent Savings and Trust. That's where the group would deliver the parcels at the end of the night, to be left unopened, as Mr. Clintock and the original members of the society had wished.

After the meeting was over and the deed was done, Bill switched cars at Woodrow's house. The Question Marks all went inside to talk about what they'd just experienced.

Sitting in the Knoxes' kitchen, eating popcorn, Woodrow asked, "Does anyone else wish we could have peeked inside the time capsules?"

"I'm totally curious," said Viola. "But I understand why they had to remain sealed."

"I don't," said Sylvester.

"Good things come to those who wait," said Rosie. "And who knows, maybe we'll be around someday when the Timekeepers decide it's time to reveal the contents."

Viola nodded. "You have to admit though, it was pretty cool to watch Ms. Dzielski open all the clocks tonight. To think that for all these years, no one knew there were secrets inside."

"And now those secrets are safe again," said Woodrow.

The Timekeepers weren't the only ones who had new business with Bill's bank that week. After nearly losing her savings, Sylvester's grandmother finally decided to start a new account. Bill helped her set up some investments, and she was happy to have the help. Woodrow was beginning to change his mind about his mom's relationship. He thought that maybe Bill was actually kind of cool, and it wasn't just because Bill had invited Woodrow to be part of his secret society. Woodrow had to admit that Bill was nice to his mom. He could be funny when he tried. And best of all, he treated Woodrow like a friend. Woodrow knew he'd been overly suspicious. He felt bad about it.

Woodrow now knew that there was only one way to win at the Strangers Game. Gather all the details you want, he thought; you still have to find out if your theories are right. To do that, despite what adults always say, you *do* have to talk to strangers. If you're lucky, later, the stranger is no longer so strange.

"What do we do now?" Viola asked, leaning back in her chair, glancing at Woodrow, Sylvester, and Rosie.

"I have an idea," said Woodrow. He leapt up from the table, then dashed out of the kitchen.

"Where's he off to?" said Rosie.

"Should we follow him?" asked Sylvester.

But before any of them could stand, Woodrow appeared in the doorway holding a large cardboard box that he'd pulled out of the recycling bin. He plopped it down on the kitchen table. Then, grabbing a pen from a drawer next to the refrigerator, Woodrow proceeded to scribble something on the box. When he was done, he showed his friends what he'd written.

the question marks mystery capsule

"I thought that maybe we could make our own. We'll each put in a few things that are important to us. Then we can seal it up and hide it away somewhere. And years from now, someone will find it and try to figure out who we were. I think it could be really cool."

Everyone agreed.

Sylvester, Rosie, and Viola rushed off to their houses to search for items to put in the box, promising Woodrow they'd be back in only a few minutes. He continued to sit at the kitchen table. He clicked the pen he'd grabbed from the drawer. He looked at it more closely, reading the words printed along the side. *One Cent Savings and Trust.* After a moment, Woodrow clicked the pen one last time. Then, very carefully, he laid it inside the cardboard box and waited for his friends to return with their own secret treasures.

ABOUT THE AUTHOR

Dan Poblocki is the author of *The Stone Child* and *The Nightmarys*. Like many writers, he's had a long list of strange jobs. Dan has traveled New Jersey as a bathing suit salesman, played the role of Ichabod Crane in a national tour of *The Legend of Sleepy Hollow*, wrangled the audience for *Who Wants to Be a Millionaire?*, sold snacks at *The Lion King*'s theater on Broadway, recommended books at Barnes & Noble, answered phones for Columbia University, and done research at Memorial Sloan-Kettering Cancer Center. He has never been a detective though, and after writing The Mysterious Four books, he thinks he might just give it a try.

Visit the author at www.danpoblocki.com.

The mysteries don't end here! Viola, Rosie, Sylvester, and Woodrow don't believe in curses — but nobody can deny that something strange is happening at Moon Hollow Middle School. Can they learn the truth before their new rivals do? Find out in . . .

THE MYSTERIOUS FOUR

MONSTERS and MISCHIEF

Available October 2011

1

THE BULLY IMPOSTER

When the final bell rang at Moon Hollow Middle
School one afternoon in late March, four friends
raced from their classrooms, not knowing that a
surprise awaited them. In separate parts of the
hallway, Sylvester, Rosie, Woodrow, and Viola
each opened their locker doors. They were too
distracted by the pieces of folded notebook paper
that fell at their feet to notice who was watching them.

They retrieved the papers and unfolded them.
Inside, written in thick black ink in the same
messy handwriting, were the words: *Meet me on
the tennis courts in five minutes. Mickey*. If someone had been listening very closely, he might have
heard strange gasping sounds as four mouths
collectively dropped open in shock.

Mickey hadn't signed his last name, but everyone already knew him. He spent most of his time
making sure his classmates knew he was the
school bully. And now, he was demanding that
the four members of the Question Marks Mystery
Club meet him in a secluded area around the
corner of the building, where a rusted fence rose

high above the cracked green surface of the so-called tennis courts. Where no one could see them from the street. It was a perfect location for an ambush.

Making eye contact with one another, Sylvester, Rosie, Woodrow, and Viola noticed the pages in one another's hands. Without exchanging any words, the four understood that they were all feeling the same thing.

Fear.